8/23/11

THE JUVENA PROJECT

WHEN A CURE FOR AGING IS DISCOVERED, THE KILLING BEGINS...

To Jane!
on the cutting edge for
medical thriller
Enjoy!

By Allan Zelinger

ISBN: 1496124278
ISBN 13: 9781496124272
Library of Congress Control Number: 2014904457
CreateSpace Independent Publishing Platform
North Charleston, South Carolina

1

Dr. Gordon Harris lay awake going over his plan, again and again. He heard a guard's footsteps outside the door then the sound of an observation slot opening and shutting. The time was 3:00 a.m.

When the footsteps faded away, Harris got up off his cot, hurried over to a storage cabinet, and took out three containers. He mixed a beaker of aluminum powder, ferrous oxide and phosphorus into a bowl. Heading to the counter, Harris grabbed several packets of sugar from near the coffee maker and emptied them into the mix. Finally, adding a small amount of water, he stirred the concoction into a sticky paste. The process complete, Harris spread gobs of it over the steel lock to the door that held him prisoner.

His decision to attempt another escape was not an easy one. This time he knew full well they would kill him if he got caught. Cautiously spacing his requests so as not to arouse suspicion, it had taken him weeks to gather the chemical components for the formula he recalled from freshman chemistry at Harvard.

Lighting a Bunsen burner, he held its flame just under the lock. Within moments, the paste reacted with a hissing sound that rapidly increased in intensity, followed by smoke and molten metal sputtering outward in all directions. Jumping back and shielding his eyes from the intense white light, Harris waited as a hole burned clear through the lock. When the fire died down, he grabbed his briefcase, kicked the smoldering door open, and ran out.

Harris had been confined in the secret basement lab for over a year. He had slept on a simple cot in the one corner that served as a living space. The rest of the room was packed with equipment for his DNA research, including a computer—although one with no connection to the outside world. When he needed something, whether a chemical reagent or a roll of toilet paper, he had to submit a written request and await its delivery by armed guard.

Gordon Harris loved the outdoors, and being cooped up nearly drove him crazy. An avid hiker who enjoyed trekking though the White Mountains of New Hampshire, he had maintained his sanity in his laboratory prison by the daily ritual of pacing briskly around the small space and doing calisthenics.

Only a few years before, the location where he had been held was still a working farm, complete with barn, stone fence, and grazing cows. The large parcel of idyllic New England countryside had since been transformed by architects and bulldozers into a complex of ultra-modern buildings belonging to the American division of a Swiss pharmaceutical company, Celestica.

Harris took a company car from the lot. He sped through a sleeping neighborhood on the way to Boston. With a tracking chip implanted in his thigh, he had to act fast. In less than an hour, a security guard would rotate by the lab again and discover that he was gone. Taking a curve too fast, his car lost traction and skidded across the street, violently striking a light pole. The impact smashed the driver-side door, shattering its window and sending glass shards flying. Harris was temporarily stunned. When he came around, the first thing he did was grope frantically behind the driver's seat. Harris was reassured when he felt the top of his briefcase. Inside it were items more important to him than his own life.

The light pole had fallen, angled across the car's hood. Amazingly, its light still functioned, brightly illuminating the vehicle's interior. Harris felt wetness on the side of his face and, looking into the mirror, saw blood oozing from a gash on his forehead. Ignoring his injury, he tried the ignition. The engine cranked but didn't turn over. He tried again, and finally the motor churned back to life. Putting the car in reverse, he pulled back. The pole rolled off the hood and dropped onto the pavement causing its giant Halogen bulb to explode like a bomb. Shifting into drive, Harris once more sped toward his destination.

It was a cool summer night and the westerly direction of wind carried moist air from the Atlantic inland, producing a thick fog that engulfed everything. Visibility was limited and Harris could barely make out a light in the distance. As he got closer, the source came into view. It was the sign for a twenty-four-hour pharmacy. Harris swerved into the store's parking lot and stopped in front of its entrance.

Inside, the lighting temporarily blinded him. Once his vision adjusted, he picked up a shopping basket and quickly proceeded down the aisles, looking for the things he needed. The store had appeared empty, but Harris soon spotted a clerk crouched behind some shelves, unpacking inventory. As Harris whisked by, the clerk politely asked, "Hey, mister, can I help you find anything?"

Harris ignored his question. He had precious little time, and didn't want to squander it engaging in banter. Flying down the aisles, he grabbed a bottle of isopropyl alcohol, roll of gauze, a sewing kit, a tube of antibiotic ointment, and a Swiss Army knife, tossing each into the basket. Stepping up to the checkout register he automatically reached for a wallet in his back pocket, but found it empty. "Damn!" Harris exclaimed, remembering it had been confiscated long ago. Without money or a credit card, he did the only thing that made sense—run out with his basket and items in hand. Taking the time to plead his predicament with the clerk could have ended up being fatal for both of them.

Harris drove on. Reaching a deserted stretch of road, he pulled over and flipped on the interior light. Undoing his belt Harris pulled down his pants. After pouring alcohol over the prominent scar on his upper thigh, he opened the pocketknife and doused its blade in alcohol. Taking a deep breath, he jabbed the sharp blade deep into his flesh, cutting parallel to the scar. A searing pain caused him to bite down hard on his lip. Spreading the incision open and using the blade as a probe, Harris gingerly worked out the chip. Once he had the blood-soaked tracking mechanism in his hand, Harris broke it into pieces and threw them out the window. Then he called out to an invisible enemy in the darkness. "You assholes won't be able to find me so easily now!"

Using the needle and thread from the sewing kit, Harris sutured the wound, bristling each time the needle penetrated his skin. Lastly, he put antibiotic ointment over the closed incision, and wrapped his thigh with gauze. Suddenly, he broke out in a cold sweat. Harris retched, but there was nothing in his stomach to give up. He had to fight hard to maintain consciousness. Using all his inner strength, Harris pulled up his trousers, shifted the car into gear, and drove off.

Although the entire makeshift operation had taken only minutes, it seemed like an eternity. Time was running short. He needed to abandon his vehicle, which could be easily identified by the company logo, a double helix of brightly colored DNA next to the word Celestica painted on its trunk. Following the sign for the Boston College T station, Harris parked the car in a corner of the lot and snatched up his briefcase. He hobbled down the stairs leading to the subway.

The Green Line was just beginning its early morning service. Harris looked around. No one was in sight. Wincing from pain, he ducked under a turnstile to gain entry. The T system, Boston's labyrinthine underground, offered countless possibilities for exiting into the city. By the time Celestica's security men found the car, Harris would be long gone. With the tracking chip removed, there was no way for them to know his precise location. He took a seat on the train, hugged the briefcase with its precious cargo on his lap, and shut his eyes. For the next twenty-five minutes, until the train reached Copley Station, Harris slept. It would be the only rest he would get that night.

2

A truck rumbled down the road leading to a village on Kinshasa's outskirts. Makebo was tending his goats when he saw a dust cloud rise in the distance. Scampering up a nearby tree gave him a better view. "My lucky day!" He exclaimed jumping down and quickly herding his flock into its enclosure. As soon as the gate shut, Makebo broke into a run for the village center. He knew what the truck meant—money. One week before, rumor had spread that a medical research team from the capital would soon be visiting.

When the vehicle halted at the central square, a side door opened and a ramp telescoped down. Workers brought out tables and chairs then set up a canopy. Technicians wearing white lab coats took their seats underneath to begin interviewing.

The fierce Congolese sun beat down on Makebo and the other waiting in line. Happily, only a few were ahead of him. A woman came by offering cold water. "Thank you," Makebo said, taking a gulp of the cool, refreshing liquid. She smiled and moved on to the next in line.

Finally, it was Makebo's turn to be interviewed. The man explained, "This is simple. We take some of your blood and check it. If the tests turn out okay, you can enroll as a research subject." Makebo nodded that he understood then looked toward the far end of the table at a cashbox filled to the brim with Congolese francs. The man showed Makebo a document. "Sign your name here if you want to be in our study." Makebo took the pen and put his signature on the line. "Very good," the man said then continued. "Now give me your arm."

After drawing three tubes of blood, the man put a dressing over the puncture site and instructed Makebo. "Don't go far. If you qualify, we'll be calling your name." Inside the truck was a mobile laboratory with scores of blood samples spinning in centrifuges that made such a din the technicians had to wear earplugs. The testing looked for evidence of HIV, hepatitis, or malaria. Only those free of previous infection could be enrolled.

Makebo sat under the shade of an enormous banyan tree with some of the other applicants. As time passed, he leaned back and looked up at the leafy canopy. He closed his eyes and soon was dreaming about the money in the cashbox. A blast from the truck's horn startled him awake. Makebo watched as a white man walked down the ramp holding a clipboard. Using a microphone, the man began reading names in a distinct British accent. "Makebo Botswana!" he called out.

Clapping his hands in joy, Makebo jumped up and strutted over to join the group of others who had qualified. Those fortunate individuals were once again led under the tent, where they waited to meet the Englishman face to face. Makebo sat across from him and watched the man open the cashbox, count out two thousand Congolese francs, and place the pile on the table directly in front of him. "Go ahead, Mr. Botswana, you can pick it up. The money is yours."

Makebo's hand quivered holding the money. The payment would easily feed and clothe his family for the entire year.

The Englishman lifted a syringe and explained to Makebo how much of the experimental medication to draw up for the daily dose. He demonstrated how Makebo should clean his skin properly with an alcohol wipe at the injection site on his thigh. When he was finished, Makebo stood anxious to leave. "Hold on there," the Englishman said, grabbing him firmly by the wrist. "Before you leave I have to watch you give yourself the first dose."

Disappointed, Makebo sat back down. He drew the proper amount of experimental milky white fluid from a vial into an empty syringe. Cleaning his skin with an alcohol swab, he injected himself, just as instructed. Afterward, Makebo requested, "Okay. Can I go now?"

"Yes, but one more thing. You must remember to keep the medication refrigerated. If it gets warm, it will spoil."

"No problem," Makebo answered.

It was late afternoon when Makebo finally returned home. His wife Tewande glared angrily at him. She was cradling the youngest of their four children in her arms, trying to comfort the crying infant. "Where have you been?" she asked. Without giving him time to answer, she continued scolding, "You never milked the goats. Their udders were about to burst. I had to do it myself."

Ignoring her, Makebo began pulling groceries from a carry sack, and laying them out on the table. Tewande was mystified. She asked, "Maki, how did you manage to get all this?" He didn't answer. Instead, reaching into his pocket, Makebo produced the wad of money for her to see.

"I don't believe it. I must be dreaming!" she exclaimed, staring at the treasure in her husband's hand. A moment later Tewande's brows furled and her jubilation evaporated. She asked in a serious tone, "Maki, you didn't steal it, did you?"

His answer came from inside the sack. He removed the vial of milky white fluid and held it up in front of her. Smiling broadly, he said one word, "Research!" Then Makebo triumphantly strutted over to the refrigerator, opened its door, and placed the vial inside.

For the next month, Makebo followed the directions given at the mobile research unit to a tee. Every morning, he injected a dose of medication from the vial under the skin of his upper thigh. One day, as he walked out of the house, Tewande called after him, "Maki, your shot. You forgot to take your shot."

He stopped and turned around. "Silly woman, I didn't forget anything. I've had enough with those damned needles. I'm no pincushion!"

"But, Maki, you signed those papers. They paid you."

"Yes, but now we have the money, and no one will ever know the difference."

Three days later, Makebo felt warm and began to perspire. A few hours later, he developed a splitting headache and started talking to people who weren't there. Somehow, he managed to stagger home. Before he could say anything, Makebo fell on the floor, convulsing, blood dripping from the corners of his mouth. Tewande screamed in fright watching her husband's uncontrollable seizure. Then she remembered the papers he had brought home after signing up for his research. Running to the cabinet she pulled them out. There was a number circled in red to call in case of emergency. Within the hour, an ambulance arrived and carted the patient out on a gurney. A medic taking Makebo's vital signs noted his temperature was 105 degrees.

The ambulance brought Makebo to a private hospital in the heart of Kinshasa. The patient was immediately rushed into a special isolation room. Samples of blood and urine were collected by two attendants covered head to toe in protective contagion suits. Before they were through, one held Makebo in fetal position while the other inserted a long needle into his back, removing several milliliters of spinal fluid for analysis. Then they packed ice bags around his body to try to bring down the high fever.

Dr. Paul Holfield stood in the hall just outside Makebo's room. He peered through a window at the sick patient and leafed through his chart. Holfield was director of clinical research for Celestica Pharmaceutical. Although he looked like a physician wearing a white lab coat he was an Oxford-educated PhD in biochemistry, not a medical doctor.

Earlier Holfield had been sitting at a favorite outdoor café, sipping coffee and contemplating the life he had led since taking up a new identity and moving from Mexico to the Congo. Holfield watched a pretty African woman walking along the thoroughfare, dressed in a colorful tight-fitting *kaba*. They made eye contact, and she waved invitingly to him. He chose to ignore her. Hookers were everywhere in Kinshasa, but at that moment Holfield was more interested in finishing his coffee than in having a woman.

Holfield's cell rang. It was Samuel Chams, his project's lead physician. "Paul, you'd better get over to the hospital right away. Another subject from our study was just admitted with severe hyperthermia."

The news hit Holfield hard and he felt his pulse quicken. "I'll be there shortly," Holfield said, trying to maintain composure in his voice. Then he added, "Make sure you send a blood sample to the lab in Geneva as soon as possible."

"Of course," Dr. Chams answered.

Holfield hung up and removed a bill from his wallet. Putting it under his unfinished cup of coffee, he hurried off to the hospital.

**

"What do you think?" Holfield asked, standing with Chams outside Makebo's room.

"I'm not quite sure," Chams answered. "At first I thought he might have cerebral malaria, but blood smears for the parasite were negative. Antibody titers for dengue fever and Ebola virus are not elevated. He's the only one in his village taken sick, so it's probably not an infectious outbreak."

"Ridiculous," Holfield interjected. "This must be some kind of infection."

An attendant went inside Makebo's room to take vitals then announced over the intercom, "His temperature is 107."

"Damn it!" Holfield blurted out. "He's burning up! Did you send off the blood sample as I requested?"

"Yes. By now I'm sure it's on the way to Geneva."

"Excellent," Holfield responded. A moment later his expression hardened. He told the physician, "I think we should move him to the morgue right away."

"What do you mean?" Chams said. "He's not dead."

"Look, Sam, you know as well as I do—the best time to identify viral particles is when they are in a stage of maximal production, and that would be now," said Holfield.

"You can't be serious about this?"

"But I am. This man is going to die regardless of anything we do. At least by performing an autopsy now, we might have the answer to what caused this. It could help prevent another case."

To appease his colleague, Holfield added, "You needn't worry. Your bonus will make up for the inconvenience. How does fifty thousand sound?"

Chams contemplated his options. Then, using the intercom, he spoke to the attendant inside. "You can go now," he said, and the man promptly left Makebo's bedside. Chams picked up a hospital phone and dialed transport. "I need a gurney sent to the isolation room, immediately." When it arrived, Chams told the orderly, "Thank you, but you can leave. I'll take it from here."

Chams and Holfield dressed in protective suits and went into Makebo's room. They lifted the patient and put him onto the cart. Holfield suggested, "Let's cover his face so he looks dead when we transport him."

"Good idea." Chams retorted, pulling a sheet from the bed and carefully draping it around the patient's body as though covering a corpse. With Holfield pushing the gurney and Chams guiding it, they headed for an elevator and took it for a short ride down to the basement to the hospital morgue.

In the refrigerated room, Holfield saw several bodies awaiting pickup for burial. Chams opened the door to an adjacent room and Holfield pushed Makebo's gurney inside. The interior was cool but not refrigerated. It was the place where autopsies were performed.

The two men put the patient onto a stainless steel table. Makebo was in a deep coma, but Dr. Chams still felt a weak pulse and saw the man's chest move with shallow respirations. From a drawer he took a syringe and filled it with a generous dose of morphine, which he injected into a vein on Makebo's forearm. Chams watched as his patient stopped breathing. Next, he took a large cutting blade from among other instruments hanging on the side of the autopsy table. Holding it up to the light he examined its sharpness. Not satisfied, Chams used a circular file, working the blade's edge, like a butcher sharpening his cleaver before slicing into a side of beef. When Chams was finished, he turned to Holfield and asked, "Are you sure you can handle this?"

"Don't worry about me," Holfield answered glibly. "A little blood and gore won't bother me."

"Okay, then, as you wish."

Chams commenced with the autopsy. He pressed his blade hard onto Makebo's upper chest, slicing across, shoulder to shoulder. Next, with a tool that looked like giant pruning shears, he divided the breastbone. Finally, he cut through the abdominal wall in the midline, all the way down from the lower end of the breastbone to as far as it could go. Opening the chest and abdominal cavities, Chams methodically removed the internal organs. He weighed each on a scale then positioned them onto a large stainless steel tray.

Using a foot pedal that activated a recorder, he dictated his findings. "The patient is a thirty-year-old male. His organs are notably discolored by numerous purple and black spots. The liver and kidneys are swollen to twice normal size and weight." Chams took his foot off the pedal, turned to Holfield, and commented, "This doesn't look like any infection I've ever seen before."

"Well, then, what the hell did this?" Holfield barked.

"I'm not sure," Chams answered. "Maybe the microscopic specimens will tell us."

Using surgical scissors, Chams took a kidney from the tray and snipped off a small piece. With a forceps, he picked up the tissue and dropped it into a glass jar filled with formaldehyde. He did the same with each of the other organs on the tray. Chams again pressed on the foot pedal. "Multiple tissue specimens were obtained for microscopic analysis from—"

"Could you hurry it up?" Holfield interrupted, feeling a wave of nausea pass through him.

"Sure," Chams answered, noticing that Holfield looked pale though the faceplate of his protective headgear. "I'll stop the dictation for now, but there's one more thing I must do."

Chams put a wooden block under Makebo's neck, elevating the head several inches off the table. He picked up a power saw and turned it on, then cut the skull circumferentially so he could remove Makebo's brain.

Holfield fought off the sick feeling that was overtaking him. Chams removed the brain from its cranial cavity. Cupping it in his hands, he walked over to Holfield. "Look how swollen the brain is. And its surface is covered with the same purple and black spots as the other organs." Holfield did everything in his power not to retch as he looked at Makebo's swollen, discolored brain. Chams carried the brain to a plastic bucket filled with preservative and placed the organ inside, saying, "After a few days in there, the soft brain tissue will firm up so I can cut it for examination."

Holfield let out a sigh of relief as the autopsy ended. They left the morgue, removed their protective outfits, and went to Chams's office. Holfield plopped down in a chair, wiping sweat from his forehead. He took gulps of cold water from a glass his host offered. "Feeling better?" Chams inquired.

Without answering, Holfield ordered, "I want you to list his cause of death as septic shock."

"Sure." Chams chortled, "I'm certainly not going to list it as morphine overdose." Finishing his paperwork, Chams paged the morgue attendant. When he called back, Chams told him, "I want you to take the body in the autopsy room to the incinerator for cremation. Be sure you wear full protective gear. The man died from a serious infection that could still be contagious."

Two days later, Makebo's ashes were brought to his wife. Holfield had a letter sent along with the remains praising him for participating in the research study and expressing sadness that he had died from an unrelated infection. A check was enclosed for five thousand Congolese francs.

It took a week for all the results from the analysis to come back. Holfield went through the file. Electron microscopy found no viral particles in the tissue. Cultures for bacteria and parasites were negative. The microscopic pathology showed blood clotted in the small arteries and multiple capillary hemorrhages. The findings suggested a case of severe heat stroke, but why should that happen?

The lab report from Geneva indicated undetectable blood levels of the experimental DNA liposomes that Makebo was supposed to have been injecting daily. His case was curiously similar to that of another research subject who had died of hyperthermia just two weeks before; that person had also had undetectable blood levels of the DNA liposomes. Suddenly, the answer struck Holfield like a bolt of lightning. Both subjects had died not from taking the experimental medication, but because they had stopped using it. That was why no liposomes had been found in their blood samples. Holfield threw Makebo's file down, then slammed his fist hard on the desk and shouted, "Fuck!"

3

Chad Reynolds was scheduled to see a dozen patients at his Boston General clinic that afternoon. All of them had conditions rarely, if ever, seen in a typical practice. Although his patients had unusual disorders, they all had one thing in common—some abnormality in their DNA. The slightest alteration in a person's DNA, just a single nucleotide out of the three billion contained within the human genome, could have dire consequences.

When Chad walked through the clinic door, his nurse Charlene looked over her glasses and greeted him. "Your first is waiting in exam room three."

Becky Robinson was a vivacious teenager afflicted with hereditary hypercholesterolemia, a one in one million disorder. Her cholesterol was 730, more than three times normal. Chad reviewed her chart, which reported the results of a recent ultrasound that showed early buildup of cholesterol plaque inside the fourteen-year-old carotid arteries supplying her brain.

He found his patient sitting on the examining table, her parents at her side. "So, how was the drive from Springfield?" Chad asked.

Her father answered with a proud smile, "We made it in record time, and without getting a ticket."

Chad responded, "You guys are really lucky. That's like winning the lottery." Despite the humor, Chad knew that Becky's father understood the gravity of his daughter's condition, which could lead to a heart attack or stroke before she had her driver's license.

"Well, I think I have some good news," Chad told them.

"Go on, Dr. Reynolds," Becky's mom chimed in. "We're all ears."

Chad continued, "Becky looks like an ideal candidate for a research study we're doing that might help."

"Please, tell us more."

"As you know, Becky has a defect in the gene coding for a liver receptor protein that binds to cholesterol and removes it from the circulation. That's why her blood levels are off the charts, and that's what's causing the premature buildup of plaque in her arteries. A former colleague of mine, Dr. Gordon Harris, discovered a way to package a critical portion of normal genes into liposomes for therapy. Liposomes are tiny, microscopic shells of harmless fat molecules," said Chad. "We would give Becky treatments with an experimental intravenous infusion of liposomes containing the normal portion of her defective liver gene's DNA. As they float through her circulation, the liposomes will be absorbed by liver cells, and release the good DNA. That should be able to help fix the problem by making normal cholesterol receptor protein."

"Dr. Reynolds, you said research, so it's experimental. Is it dangerous? And have you had any results so far?" asked Becky's father.

"So far, in the three patients enrolled, we saw cholesterol levels drop into a safe range."

Her mother asked, "Any side effects?"

Chad answered, "None so far."

"Wow," Becky interjected. "That sounds terrific."

"You bet it does, but it's still a bit early to be sure whether the benefits will hold up. Only time will tell."

"What's our next step?" Becky's father inquired.

"If you are interested, I'll set up a meeting with our research coordinator to go over details. Once you agree and sign the consent forms, we can begin the infusions," Chad said. "Remember, folks, there is no guarantee. I don't want to build up false hopes."

"Understood," said Becky's father.

**

At 6:00 p.m., as Chad's last patient was departing, he glanced out a window at the setting sun. He told his nurse, "Char, I think I'll finish my charting at home." With that, Chad scooped up some files from the counter and stuffed them in his briefcase.

Charlene began, "Dr. Reynolds, don't forget..." but before she could finish her statement, he was out the door.

4

Chad had burst into his Back Bay apartment. He desperately wanted to get in a run before dark. Tossing his briefcase on the sofa and heading straight for the bedroom, he exchanged work clothes for shorts and a T-shirt. Taking care of sick children and their anxious parents was stressful. Running was his therapy. Slipping on his running shoes, Chad bolted down the stairs, hitting the pavement full out. He ran west on Marlboro Street to Mass Avenue, then north, crossing the bridge over the Charles River to Cambridge. He continued along the riverbank track until he reached the Harvard Boat House then turned around to head back.

As the sun dropped lower in the sky, it cast a mystical crimson hue over the stately brownstones across the river on Beacon Hill. A rowing squad was sculling parallel to Chad as he ran. It was July, and even though the academic year was over, dedicated crew teams continued to practice. Chad watched their oars cut through the water in unison as the coxswain barked out a cadence.

Chad wiped sweat from his brow and was breathing hard on the last leg of his route. He had moved to Boston from Chicago for his pediatric residency at the General. Chad had only been to Boston once before that, on the day of his interview, when his experience of the city consisted of the short cab ride from Logan airport to the hospital and back. However, it hadn't taken him long once he lived there to fall in love with Boston. Now there was nowhere else he'd rather be.

As Chad proceeded down Marlboro toward his apartment, his thoughts turned to Kristen. That week she was away in Cleveland, visiting her parents. Like Chad, Kristen was a transplant to Boston. She had had gotten her journalism degree at Boston University and, after graduating, taken a job at the *Globe*. The two of them had met during a hospital fundraiser held at the Gardner, a museum housed in a large mansion originally built in the style of a fifteenth-century Venetian palazzo. As Chad ambled around the expansive mansion, he spotted an auburn-haired beauty in front of *El Jaleo*, holding a glass of wine and silently contemplating Sargent's magnificent life-size painting.

"Amazing piece," Chad said, attempting to get her attention.

"Yes, it is," she said, turning to him. Her smile and sparkling green eyes instantly captivated Chad.

"The Gypsy dancer in the picture makes you feel like you're in Spain, not Boston," said Chad.

"No question. The painting is so real it draws you in."

"By the way, my name is Chad Reynolds. I'm one of the pediatric docs at the General."

"Kristen Ross," she answered, extending her hand. "I'm a writer at the *Globe*. I heard about the event from a friend who was supposed to meet me here." Glancing down at her watch, she continued. "I guess something must have come up, because that was almost an hour ago."

"Well, I'm happy to keep you company, if it's okay?"

Kristen blushed. "That would be really nice."

The Gardner event had been over two years ago and Chad remained just as smitten as on their first meeting. Although they had broached the topic of marriage, for now both were more focused on their careers.

Kristen was a unique personality with unusual skills to match: she was an accomplished third-degree black belt in karate. The collection of trophies scattered throughout their apartment attested to her ability. It always struck Chad as interesting that someone so thoroughly feminine had such great passion for a martial art. One evening over dinner and wine he asked, "Kristen, what's with the karate thing? How did you get ever get into it?"

She answered, "Okay, here's the awful truth. I started out in ballet, but I was so bad…I mean really pathetic. One day I walked past a karate class going on down the hall and the students looked so into what they were doing I decided to give it a shot. It wasn't long after, that I traded in my ballet slippers and leotard for bare feet and a *gi*. The rest is history."

After her repeated requests, Chad attempted to take up the discipline. However, he left his second session with bruised ribs and the belief that as much as he cared for Kristen, karate was not for him. Chad was six feet tall, with a muscular build and stood nearly a head taller than her. Yet, half-kidding with friends, Chad would say he was afraid to go into the tougher neighborhoods of Boston without taking Kristen along for protection.

Running wasn't Kristen's favorite pastime but she occasionally accompanied Chad and was in good enough shape to keep pace. The evening before her Cleveland trip, she had joined in. Returning to their apartment, spent and sweating, Chad lobbied for a quick dinner out. "Are you hungry?" he asked.

"I'm famished."

"How about we go to that new sushi place on Newbury?"

"Sounds nice, but I really don't have much time. I need to finish the outline on one of my projects and I haven't even packed for my trip."

"Don't worry, sushi doesn't take long. Come on. Let's jump in the shower together. It'll speed things up."

Kristen thought for a moment, and then acquiesced, "Okay, I'll go."

Their clothes were off in a flash and to save time they both squeezed into the shower barely large enough for two. As she soaped Chad's back, one of Kristen's hands journeyed downward, to his thigh. He felt the softness of her breasts pressing against him. Her cue had its intended effect.

He turned around. "I thought you were in a hurry?"

Her answer was a deep kiss on his mouth. Kristen's tongue playfully met Chad's. As warm water rinsed the soap off their bodies, they made love. They never made it to Newbury Street.

5

When Chad entered the apartment after his post-clinic run, he was confronted by silence. Kristen's absence was soon painfully evident. He longed to see her and hear the sound of her voice. Dropping onto the sofa, he dialed her phone but got no answer. After showering, he sat at his desk to work on the clinic charts. Later, at the kitchen table, he unexcitedly picked at his food while going through the day's mail. It was getting late but he still hadn't heard back from Kristen. He moved to the sofa and began reading one of the many medical journals accumulating atop his coffee table. In no time, he was asleep sitting up, the open magazine on his lap.

Chad awoke with a start to the sound of his apartment buzzer going off. He found himself lying stretched out on the sofa where he had fallen asleep reading. Chad rubbed his eyes and looked at his watch. The time was 4:15 a.m. At first he tried to ignore the buzzer, figuring it must be some mistake or prank. Rolling over, he was back to sleep in seconds. Then the buzzer went off again. "Damn it!" Chad yelled, jumping up off the sofa to see who was rudely interrupting his sleep.

He hollered into the intercom, "What's your problem ass—," but before finishing the tirade, a familiar voice interrupted.

"Chad, I'm sorry to wake you up at this ungodly hour. But could you please, let me in?"

"Jesus! Dr. Harris! Forgive me. I had no idea…." Pressing the button to open his entry door, Chad responded. "My place is at the top of the stairs, second one to your right." Chad stepped into the dimly lit hallway and waited. Walking toward him, carrying his trademark weathered satchel briefcase was Dr. Gordon Harris.

No person had been more important to Chad's career than Harris, an MD PhD, world-renowned authority on human genetics, and his *ex officio* department head. Chad hadn't seen him since the day Harris had abruptly left his position at the General more than a year ago. However, the man standing at in his doorway hardly resembled the Gordon Harris of old. His pepper-gray hair was disheveled and his face overdue for a shave. There was a gash with dried blood on his forehead.

"Dr. Harris, please come in." Noticing the limp and blood on his mentor's slacks, Chad said, "What happened? You're hurt."

"Oh, it's only minor—nothing serious. And please no formalities. Call me Gordon." In truth, Harris's leg throbbed with pain, and he practically fell onto the sofa in the living room. "I know I must look like hell. Unfortunately, I don't have much time before I have to leave."

"Gordon, what is it?"

Harris looked directly at Chad and said, "My friend, I could really use your help."

"Of course, anything," Chad answered. "The last I heard from you was the letter from Switzerland, and that was over a year ago. You wrote that you had taken that position at some Swiss biotech company, but gave no address, e-mail, or phone number. I had no way to contact you."

Harris winced, changing position. "A lot has happened during the last year, but one thing is for certain—I never left the country, or even Massachusetts."

"What? Chad blurted in utter disbelief. "The note you sent was postmarked from Switzerland. You can look at it yourself. I've kept it in my desk."

Chad stood up to get it but Harris motioned him back. "Chad, you needn't bother. I'm sure you're correct. They forced me to write that phony letter and must have couriered it abroad then posted it back to make it look as though I sent it from Switzerland."

Chad was confused. "Gordon, I don't understand."

Harris answered, "I know this is going to sound crazy, but from the time I disappeared suddenly until tonight, I have been held against my will at a research facility west of Framingham."

Chad's was stunned by Harris's claim.

"Have you ever heard of Celestica Pharmaceutical?" asked Harris.

"Sure. Who hasn't? It's one of the biggest pharma houses in Europe."

"That's right," Harris said. "Their headquarters is in Geneva, Switzerland, but they have a new American division near Framingham. I was held captive in one of the buildings on their property until escaping just a few hours ago."

"You escaped…?"

"Yes," Harris answered. Glancing at his watch he said, "I've got to get going. But first, I have some things that need safe keeping. Can I give them to you?"

"Of course, Gordon, but don't you think you should go to the police?" said Chad. "Come on. I can drive you there right now."

"No," Harris said. "I'd love to go to the police, but I just can't do that—at least not yet. There isn't enough time now to explain."

Harris stood, groaning as he put full weight on the injured leg, and lifted his satchel onto the coffee table. Opening it, he took out a computer disk labeled "Juvena Project." He handed the disk to Chad, and then reached in again. This time he removed a Plexiglas cube holding three white mice huddled together in a corner. He set the cube on the table. Finally, Harris pulled out a small Styrofoam container. He pried off the lid and opened the container just enough to pull out a small vial. A cold white mist from the dry ice puffed out when he closed the lid. "Chad, these vials contain very special DNA liposomes. It's essential that these three mice get a daily injection if they are to remain alive. It's just as important to keep the vials cold. Heat denatures them and they lose their effectiveness."

"Mice? This is about mice? I don't get it."

Harris carried the small cage over to Chad's desk and held it up to the light. "As you know, lab mice typically live for about two years. These mice are quite different. They come from a strain I genetically modified to age prematurely. I bioengineered them with the mouse equivalent of progeria, the human disorder of premature aging."

"Like the kids with progeria you saw in your clinic?"

"Precisely like them," Harris answered.

**

Harris was a leading international expert on Hutchinson-Gilford syndrome, more commonly known as progeria, the rare lethal disorder of accelerated aging. Parents from all over the world with children affected by this one in a million disorder sought out Harris's expertise. Sadly, there was precious little he could do; the young patients invariably died of old-age maladies before they reached adulthood.

Harris smiled at Chad and said with satisfaction, "I finally have something to help those kids, and it's in those vials. Come take a close look at these progeria mice. Given their genetic defect, their life expectancy is only three to four months, but all of them are now well over twelve months old. They don't show any of the usual signs you'd expect in aging mice, like losing teeth or a thinning coat of hair. And look: the female appears to be even younger than the two males."

Chad peered at the mice closely. "No question. She's got to be much younger."

"Your observation is correct, but you might be surprised to learn that she is the mother of the other two! I began administering the DNA liposomes to her a few weeks before the offspring, creating an aging paradox within the family. There's something else I found."

"What's that?"

"When you administer these DNA liposomes to normal mice, you slow aging to a near standstill."

Chad looked at the mice, then toward Harris. It seemed too good to be true. Harris anxiously checked his watch again. "Damn, I'm overstaying my visit."

Chad interjected, "For God's sake, Gordon, why didn't you let me know about this when you were still at the General?"

Harris answered, "I didn't want to raise false hopes. I hate talking about work that's incomplete, and I had more verification to do. And then the Celestica bastards took me."

"How did they find out about your research? How did you get involved with Celestica?"

"Well, my research funding dried up. Apparently the NIH didn't think an orphan disorder like progeria, which affects so few, merited continuing financial support. They terminated my grant. By sheer chance one Sunday morning I happened to read a newspaper article about a pharmaceutical company that was interested in acquiring promising new locally developed drugs. It was Celestica. I wondered if they might be willing to fund my work, so I called them. Eventually, I met with a man named Jim Anderson, the company's regional manager. I brought along my progeria mice and made a pitch for funding."

Harris's expression soured. "Unfortunately, Anderson had other intentions for my research. He didn't care about treating progeria. He wanted to use my DNA liposomes as a way to slow aging and keep people young. The commercialized treatment would be the company's new blockbuster. Anderson offered me three million dollars to sign over the rights. Of course, I refused—and that's when they came after me. Celestica is ready to begin marketing just as soon as they get regulatory approval on the drug. They call it Juvena, after the Roman god of youth."

Chad was speechless. Harris continued, "Now, they want me and those mice back. And you can take my word for it—they will do anything to do it. I'm certain they won't hesitate to kill again. There are billions of dollars at stake."

Chad's couldn't believe his ears. "Gordon, did you say kill?"

"I did. They have killed already," said Harris. "And if I stay any longer, it could put you in danger, too."

"But, Gordon—"

Harris interrupted. "Chad, I'm sure you have more questions. I'll find some way to safely get in touch with you, but until then, please assume that you are being watched. The company is sure to keep an eye on my old associates, looking for any contact."

As Chad's nocturnal guest was about to leave he delivered a final message. "Please take good care of those mice. On the surface they might not look so special, but there aren't three others like them anywhere in the world."

Harris began hobbling toward the door. Then he turned to say, "Oh, one more thing. They took all my money and credit cards. I don't even have an ID. Can you possibly loan me some cash?"

"Sure I can." Chad answered. Taking out his wallet, he handed Harris all the money. Then Chad told him, "Here, Gordon, take my ATM card in case you need more." Writing down his code he gave it to Harris with the card.

"I can't thank you enough." Harris told his friend. "Someday I'll find a way to repay you for all your help."

With those words, Dr. Gordon Harris, world famous geneticist and Chad's former department head, left the apartment.

Chad's world had been just been shaken to the core. Despite the incredulous story, his gut told him that Harris spoke the truth.

It was 4:45 a.m. when Chad put the vials in the refrigerator. As he lay down in bed, he pondered Harris's refusal to go to the police. *If he really was a prisoner, and he believes those people will kill—or have killed—what would keep him from reporting it? Why not go straight to the cops?* Unable to come up with an answer that made sense, Chad fell into a restless sleep for the short time that remained of a very strange night.

6

Rolfe Witig had a splitting headache. He took a pain pill then swallowed it with a gulp of mineral water. He'd had occasional headaches for years, but now there was good reason for their increase. As the CEO of Celestica Pharmaceutical, he had watched the company drop in a downward financial spiral despite all of his best efforts. Bad luck and a few questionable decisions had brought his once-thriving company to the brink of insolvency.

The drug QB-163 had nearly destroyed it. To bolster Celestica's pipeline, Witig had convinced his board to spend six hundred million buying the rights to an exciting new compound, then another two hundred million to run the clinical trials required to get the European Medicines Agency seal of approval. All tallied, they had spent nearly a billion on QB-163, which was later named Quellinol by the marketing department.

The drug represented a whole new way to achieve pain control without the risks associated with many other pain-killers, so it was well worth the expense. Before the purchase, Witig had even tried the drug himself when he had one of his headaches. After he took QB-163, his pain had disappeared within minutes, and without making him fatigued the way his narcotic medication did. He was sold. At the meeting of his board, Witig gave them his personal testimonial, and easily garnered enough votes to purchase rights to the new wonder drug.

The day the European Medicines Agency approved Quellinol, Celestica's stock price had shot up thrity-five percent. That was followed by a flurry of investment upgrades, and the stock price climbed even higher. Witig, his board of directors, and his family members, owning the lion's share of Celestica stock, were all elated. Distant relatives phoned from St. Moritz, Bern, Paris, Nice, and Monte Carlo, all congratulating him as they saw their personal fortunes rise with the company's stock price. Witig was their new savior.

His next goal was getting approval from the USFDA. He spent countless hours dealing with the necessary documentation. Witig was sure he could get Quellinol approval in the United States within a few months of its European launch. With his new product about to land on pharmacy shelves in the United States, his company was poised for an astounding financial windfall. Then Witig could achieve something he had dreamed about—the takeover of Novara, a rival Swiss pharmaceutical company he'd had his eye on for years.

Unfortunately, the worst possible thing happened. Just four months after Quellinol hit European pharmacy shelves, bad news started filtering in. The first reported case of liver problems in a patient taking Quellinol was followed by a second, just a week later. Not long after that, a third. Once the first patient died of liver failure, all hell broke loose.

The media erupted with disparaging stories about Quellinol. After seeing the *Financial Times* headline, "Celestica's Revolutionary Pain-Killer Kills," Witig developed severe chest pain and was rushed to the hospital by ambulance. Luckily, tests showed his heart was fine, and he was discharged home two days later, a phalanx of reporters following in hot pursuit.

The media alleged that corporate greed had led to inadequate research before getting the drug's approval, but Witig knew that nothing could be further from the truth. He had spent a bloody fortune testing the drug, and there was never a hint of liver problems. Human studies on Quellinol had been meticulously conducted by the company's director of clinical research, Paul Holfield, PhD, a man with impeccable academic credentials.

It turned out that the liver cases occurred only in patients who were also heavy consumers of alcohol. Such people had been excluded from the study population, but that didn't matter. The European regulators forced Celestica to take Quellinol off the market rather than permit its continued use even with the proposed addition of warnings against alcohol consumption on its labels and packaging.

As Witig sat at his desk waiting for his headache to subside, he realized that all hope for the company's future now rested on Juvena. Approval of the revolutionary anti-aging treatment was vital. As he pondered Celestica's turnaround, his administrative secretary, Inger, spoke over the intercom. "Herr Witig, can you take a call from Mr. Anderson? He says it's urgent."

"Go ahead. Put him through."

Witig glanced over at the international clock on his desk. "Jim, isn't it's a bit early for you to be at work? It's six in the morning over there."

"Actually, Rolfe, I'm at home. I really hate to tell you this but I just received a call from Murdock. He says Dr. Harris has escaped."

"What? That's impossible. I thought you had him locked up."

"We did, but he managed to get out."

"Shit!" Witig exclaimed.

"Fortunately, I don't think it will take long before we get him back. We are monitoring his location using a tracking chip implanted in his body," Anderson lied. He knew from Murdock that the chip signal had gone dead several hours earlier.

"Can you get to him before he goes to the police?"

"I don't think we have to worry about Harris going to the authorities. A cold-blooded murderer isn't likely to ask the police for help."

"You're right. For a moment, I forgot." Witig continued. "But, please remember: when you find him, don't kill him. Harris is still more important to us alive, at least until Juvena is approved by the USFDA. After that you can do with him as you wish."

"Of course, Herr Witig," Anderson answered respectfully.

Witig put the receiver down. Despite the assurance, he felt unsettled. Harris's brilliance represented a potential danger. From behind his massive desk, Witig shouted, "Damn it, Anderson, you'd better not screw this up!"

Witig spoke to Inger. "No calls for the next hour."

"As you wish, my dear," she answered.

The news about Harris didn't help Witig's headache. The searing pain behind his eyes was worse. He took another Quellinol from the supply he still kept for personal use and swung his chair around until he faced a wall filled with framed panels of vividly colored alpine flowers. Witig collected these on his mountain treks. The blue gentian, purple androsace, white edelweiss, and pink alpenrose brought life to an otherwise stark office. Witig always found it soothing to view them. He rested his head back and closed his eyes.

**

Witig had a deep love for the mountains where he had grown up. He owned a chalet in Grindelwald that he used as a base for local treks, and went on at least one major climbing expedition every year. Witig was a member of a select group of accomplished mountaineers to have taken on the world's most difficult peaks, and he loved looking down on the earth from summits he risked his life to ascend. His best moments had been those spent far above the tree line. His Everest climb four years earlier had been the ultimate. Nothing compared to the moment when he looked down on China, India, Tibet, and Nepal from 29,028 feet up. More than four thousand people attempt Everest's summit every year, but only a fraction actually make it to the top, and he was one of them. On his desk sat the photo of him and Nygen, his Sherpa guide, together atop Everest's peak. It was Witig's most prized possession.

**

The intercom came on, awakening him. "I must have dozed off," Witig said to Inger over the speaker.

"Johann Maurer is here for his three o'clock appointment."

"Okay, send him in." Witig quickly straightened his shirt and tie. He was thankful that his headache had abated during the nap. Maurer was president of Swiss Bank in Bern. He had recently reconfigured Celestica's massive loans, helping Witig maintain the company's solvency.

"My dear friend, Rolfe," Johann said, extending his hand as he entered the office.

"You mean, 'dear friend,' as long as I continue to pay the interest on our outstanding debt."

"Well, that's putting it bluntly, but frankly...quite correctly." Maurer and Witig laughed as they shook hands.

"Well, I promised you an update on our Juvena project, didn't I?" Witig asked. "Fortunately, the good news is that the documentation necessary for the European Medicines Agency approval of Juvena is nearly complete. After that, we will bring it before the USFDA. Soon, I will have the number one pharmaceutical blockbuster of the decade in our arsenal."

"And what is the likelihood that the agency will rule favorably?"

"Approval is a certainty," Witig answered.

"That's music to my banker ears," Johann chortled.

"But, let me warn you—once the money starts pouring in from sales of Juvena, I will be calling on you again," said Witig.

"You still want to buy Novara, don't you?"

"Yes. I've been waiting patiently for a very long time. If not for the unexpected problem with Quellinol, it would already have been a done deal."

There was a knock at the door. When it opened, Inger pushed in a cart with champagne and caviar. "A little treat," she said smiling at Witig and Johann.

Inger poured the champagne. They raised their glasses. Witig smiled broadly and toasted, "To our success with Juvena!"

7

C had awoke wishing the night before had been just a bad dream. However, the satchel on his coffee table was proof it wasn't. He prepared for work in a daze. Before leaving the apartment, he repacked Harris's briefcase with the mice, vials of Juvena, and the computer disk. At the General's research building, he unlocked the lab office that had once belonged to Harris and had since been reassigned to him. After setting the briefcase down on his desk, Chad stopped to look at a photo mounted on the wall. It showed Harris standing in the center of a group of young doctors, including himself—his graduating class of pediatric residents from Boston General. Next to that hung a handsome plaque certifying his completion of a fellowship at John Hopkins in genetic disorders. Gordon Harris's glowing letter of recommendation had helped him land that highly coveted fellowship spot.

A moment later Chad was lost in a memory of sitting in the General's gargantuan lecture hall while Dr. Harris gave a talk to a packed house. Harris put up the slide of a frail, elderly man. What little hair he had left was white. The man was hunched over and held a cane. Harris turned to the crowd. "Let me take a vote," he said. "How many here think this person is under eighty?" No hands went up. "How many think he's over eighty?" A sea of hands shot up.

"Unfortunately," Harris told the audience, "he happens to be one of my patients with progeria. He just celebrated his tenth birthday." The audience in the lecture hall collectively gasped.

Having captured his audience's interest, Harris went on to review basic concepts in the process of aging.

"Living cells," he said, "have a finite capacity to divide and form new copies, known as the Hayflick limit. The number of cell divisions is thought by some to determine the lifespan of an organism. When our cells run out of their ability to divide, we are nearing end of the line." Harris clicked through a number of slides.

"Other studies have shown that diet is an important factor. Animals fed low-calorie diets, basically the semi-starvation diet of basic sustenance, live longer than those fed normally. This suggests a link between cellular metabolism and aging. Metabolism has the obligatory byproduct of free radicals. Those free radicals can damage cell structures and, in doing so, contribute to aging. It's like oxidizing internally. Some people believe we rust to death." The audience chuckled appreciatively.

"Then there's the telomere theory." Harris put up a slide of a magnified chromosome with one end illuminated. "The bright tip on this chromosome is its telomere. These are located at the N-terminal portion on each of the forty-six chromosomes in our cells. Telomeres shorten until they reach a point at which the process becomes irreversible, a point of programmed cell death known as *apoptosis*." He projected another image. "Perhaps I should also remind you that telomeres play a role in cancer. Their malfunction can sometimes permit uncontrolled cell division resulting in a malignant tumor that could live on forever except for one detail. The tumor will inevitably die when it kills its host."

Harris summarized. "These are some of the current theories about aging. However, none totally explains the process in its entirety. However, if we really understood what caused the premature aging in our ten-year-old patient, the boy whose slide I showed earlier, the mystery of our ticking biological clocks would finally be unlocked. Progeria is a horrible disorder, but provides us with an accident of nature we can learn from. I encourage all of you who are interested to consider research in this area. One day, it might be one of you in today's audience who will find the cure for this atrocious malady."

**

Chad's reverie ended abruptly when his pager went off. He called the extension and his resident answered, "Dr. Reynolds, we're in the conference room waiting to make rounds. Are you coming?

"Yes, of course. I'll be there in a few minutes." From the brief-case, he removed the Plexiglas container that held Harris's mice and placed it among the many identical containers housing his own experimental rodents. Lastly, Chad put the vials of Juvena in the lab refrigerator. Locking the lab door behind him, he hurried to the hospital to meet up with his team.

8

Harris's nightmare had begun a year earlier, when he turned down Celestica's "generous" offer for rights to his DNA liposomes. Anderson had phoned Switzerland. "Rolfe, Harris refused to sign with us."

"You mean the greedy doctor wants *more* than three million?"

"No, money isn't the issue. He is against manipulating genes unless there is a disorder involved. Progeria qualifies, but normal aging doesn't."

"Look, Jim, I don't give a damn what Harris believes in. I want those liposomes for Celestica. Do whatever you have to do to get him to sign. Understand?"

"Yes, Herr Witig," Anderson answered as his boss hung up.

Anderson sat at his desk, thinking. He knew someone who might be able to help. Picking up the phone he called Bill Murdock.

**

An uneventful week had passed since Harris's meeting with Anderson. It was late evening when he left the General, walking home to his apartment on Beacon Hill. A bachelor, Harris was married to the work he loved—work that so totally consumed him that it left no space for a longstanding relationship. Instead, Harris was sentenced to settle for short-term affairs that generally ended when the woman discovered the unwinnable nature of her competition, his work.

Harris often ate dinner at the hospital or at a restaurant. He especially liked frequenting the Shamrock, an Irish pub located just down the street from the General. That evening when he entered through the Shamrock's front door, the sound of live music filled the air. A popular local band was playing Irish ballads. The atmosphere was festive.

Harris took a seat at an empty table. A few minutes later, an unfamiliar server approached. She wore a tight red skirt, with a blouse unbuttoned to reveal ample cleavage.

"Evening," she said, "my name is Claire. Can I offer you something to drink?"

"Sure, I'll have a Guinness."

When Claire returned with his beer, she bent down in a way that placed her breasts directly in front of Harris's face. He had no choice but to get an eyeful. "And have you decided what you'd like for dinner?"

"I think I'll go with the shepherd's pie."

"Great choice," she said, nodding in approval.

By the time she came with his meal, he had polished off the pint of Guinness. "Want another?" Claire asked, setting down his plate.

"Sure, why not?" Harris answered. "It's supposed to be good for your heart."

"Honey," she replied. "Guinness is good for everything."

Later, when he was done eating, Claire brought his bill. She surprised Harris by sitting down next to him. "What about stopping over at my place for another drink before you head home?"

Harris balked. "I don't know...I've got to get up early tomorrow for work. Staying up late is probably not such a good idea."

"Who said we have to stay up?" Claire said. She whispered in his ear, "I'll make it worth your while." Claire pressed her soft breasts against his arm while her hand touched his inner thigh.

Harris acquiesced. "Well, I guess one more drink won't hurt."

When they arrived at her apartment, Claire poured him a scotch and added the powder Murdock had given her. As Harris drank, she turned on some music and set the lights low. She sat next to him on the sofa. Claire wore no bra and Harris's face was soon between her breasts, kissing and caressing. She took his hand and put it between her legs. She wasn't wearing any underwear. Harris's heart was pounding. He was done with foreplay if she was. Claire got up and undid her skirt, letting it drop to the floor. She was standing naked in front of him. "Come on, honey, let's go to the bedroom."

When Harris tried to stand, his legs wouldn't support him. He started laughing, and said, "I guess I had a little too much to drink."

"Let me give you a hand," Claire offered, reaching out to help him. With her support, he managed to make it into the bedroom.

"Jeez, I'm dizzy," Harris said, slurring his words. Claire sat him down on the bed's edge, unbuckled his belt, and then pulled off his slacks. Harris had a difficult time speaking and couldn't coordinate his arm movements. The erection he had had minutes before was gone. Now Claire was laughing, and he was confused. A moment later he fell backward, onto the bed, unconscious.

Claire made a call on the cell phone she had been given by the man who had arranged the evening, giving her a set of keys and the address of the apartment she'd told Harris was hers. Murdock had also given her an envelope filled with hundred-dollar bills, promising her an equal amount when she was through with the job.

Within minutes of receiving her call, Murdock, Celestica's head security consultant, showed up at the apartment. He walked over to the bed and looked down at the unconscious Harris. "Sweet dreams," he said with a sneer. Then he turned to Claire, who was putting her clothes back on. "Nice work. I knew I could count on you."

"Thanks. Now, if you don't mind, can I have the rest of my money?"

"Sure, it's right here," he said, tapping an area on his sport coat. He reached inside, pulled out the envelope, and handed it to her.

Claire sat down on the bed and counted her fee. "Looks like the money's all here," she said with a smile. "Where's the other stuff you promised?"

"Oh, yes," he said, acting like he'd forgotten. Murdock pulled out a clear plastic bag containing white powder. Inside was more heroin than Claire had ever seen before at one time.

"Where'd you get all that?" she asked, but didn't wait for an answer. She grabbed the bag out of his hand.

Murdock didn't tell her that it wasn't the weakened street drug she was used to. The heroin Claire bought on the street was cut by each intermediary in the supply chain; by the time it finally reached her, the white powder was mostly filler. Murdock had taken this drug from Celestica's chemical reagent store-room; the powder in the bag was 99.9 percent pure heroin.

Claire couldn't wait to shoot up. She opened her purse and took out some paraphernalia. Murdock watched in silence. Claire's hands were trembling as she asked, "Can you help me out? I don't want to make a mess."

"It would be my pleasure." Murdock answered taking the spoon and putting some heroin at its base. He estimated it was only about a gram, but at that purity, it was many times the lethal dose. He heated the spoon with a lighter until the powder turned to liquid, and drew it up into the syringe. Claire, busy tightening the tourniquet around her upper arm to plump up her veins, was too distracted and excited to ask Murdock why he was wearing latex gloves. Claire took the syringe from Murdock, her hand surprisingly steady as it neared the access to her bloodstream. Injecting the drug, she loosened the band around her upper arm using her teeth.

Claire moaned in ecstasy. "This is some good shit—" she said. Then her eyes rolled back and she collapsed onto the bed next to Harris, the needle still sticking in her arm. Murdock looked down at her, watching her lips and face turn a progressively darker shade of blue. Her breathing became barely detectable then stopped. The dose of pure heroin was more than enough to paralyze her brainstem's respiratory drive. Murdock reached down to feel her carotid. She had no pulse.

Murdock picked the envelope of money and put it back into his pocket. He spilled heroin powder over Harris's body. Next, Murdock picked up the phone he had given Claire and made a call. "You can come on up now," he told his associate. Then Murdock placed the cell phone on the nightstand and waited.

He heard a knock at the door and let Earl Flowers in. When the new arrival saw Harris and Claire lying naked on the bed he said, sarcastically, "Nice, very nice. They make a handsome couple, don't they?"

"Yes, they do," Murdock said. Flowers stood by the bed, staring. "Enough gawking," Murdock snapped. "There's plenty of work to be done. Let's be quick about it."

Flowers opened his bag, took out a digital camera then mounted it on a tripod. Next he removed all of Claire's clothing. Flowers began taking a series of incriminating photos with the naked dead girl and drugged doctor positioned like they were having sex. Lastly, he took a shot of Claire's arm as it lay across Harris's chest with a heroin filled syringe, its needle still sticking in her vein.

Flowers hid a small microphone behind the nightstand that would tell him when Harris awoke. He removed the memory chip from the camera but left the empty camera and tripod in place. "Too bad we won't be able to see the look on his face when he wakes up with the dead girl next to him."

"Well, who the fuck cares about that? I just hope he doesn't have a heart attack and croak on us." Murdock looked down at Harris. "Anyway, you got to feel a little sorry for the poor bastard."

"What? *You* feel sorry for someone. That'd be a first."

Murdock took a second to look back at the two people on the bed. "You're right. I don't feel sorry."

They left the apartment slapping each other on the back in congratulations for a job well done.

**

William Murdock had started his career with good intentions. He had dedicated his life to God and Country. A graduate with honors from West Point, he'd spent combat time in Afghanistan. However, seeing his friends torn to shreds by RPGs and road-side bombs changed him. He began doing things that weren't covered in the rules of engagement. When Murdock wanted to know something really important from a prisoner, he wouldn't waste time with conventional interrogation. Instead, he would take the man for a ride in a chopper. Ascending high above the desert, beyond the reach of the Geneva Convention, Murdock would hang the prisoner outside, head down. Once the enemy spilled everything—and it wouldn't take long—Murdock cut the cord. The method made information-gathering a quick, clean process. The sands below swallowed the evidence.

After he left the military, Murdock went into the private security business, starting a company called SSC, Special Security Consultants. His reputation for doing whatever it took to get a job done was why Anderson had hired him to handle the delicate situation with Harris.

9

When he opened his eyes, Harris found himself starring up at a strange ceiling. He was groggy and disoriented. Harris felt something on top of his chest. Looking down it surprised him to find a woman's arm. Propping himself up on one elbow he saw the arm belonged to a naked lady lying in bed next to him. Her face was turned away and she appeared to be deeply asleep. Suddenly, parts of the previous evening began flooding back into his consciousness.

He remembered the pub…the waitress, Claire…going to her apartment…then, nothing. Harris whispered, "Claire?" but she didn't respond. He nudged her—still no response. Then he saw the needle stuck in her arm.

Harris sat up so he could look at her face. Claire's eyes were open, staring ahead, and not moving. Her lips were blue. She wasn't breathing. "Oh, shit!" Harris screamed. He turned her over, then frantically began pumping on her chest and giving her mouth-to-mouth. He stopped to feel for a pulse. There was nothing. She was dead.

Harris saw a bag of white powder lying on the nightstand along with a spoon and lighter. With the needle in her arm and drugs on the nightstand, it could only mean one thing. She had taken an overdose.

His heart was pounding so hard he thought it would jump out of his body. Harris looked down at his own naked body. He had white powder all over his chest and abdomen. "Oh my God!" he cried out.

What should he do? Get dressed and leave? Call the police? Harris was paralyzed by indecision. Then a cell phone on the nightstand rang.

Cautiously, he picked it up, hand trembling. Harris didn't say anything; he couldn't speak. Instead, he listened as a man's voice spoke with a reassuring tone. "Dr. Harris, please don't panic. The woman with you is obviously dead, and there is nothing that can be done for her. If you look beyond the foot of the bed, you will see a camera mounted on a tripod." Harris glanced over and saw the camera. The voice asked, "Do you see it?"

"Yes," Harris answered.

"Well, I have a memory chip filled with pictures of you and the dead woman together. The lighter, the spoon, and the syringe sticking out of her arm have your fingerprints all over them. As far as the police would be concerned, you injected the drug that killed her," Murdock said. "That makes you at the very least an accomplice in her death. You would spend a considerable time in jail, and when they let you out as a convicted felon, you wouldn't be able to practice medicine again."

Murdock paused to let Harris digest the information. "And don't think that taking the syringe and running away will help. I have another one with your fingerprints on it, for safekeeping."

"Who are you? Why...why are you doing this?"

"Never mind that for now. All you need to know is that I can make your problem go away. I can make the mess you are in now disappear like it never happened. You'd like that, wouldn't you?"

Harris answered, speaking softly. "Yes."

"That's good, Dr. Harris. You've made the right decision. Now, please put your clothes on. Leave everything in the apartment as it is. A black sedan will pull up in front of the building five minutes from now. Get inside." Then the line went dead.

For a minute, Harris sat frozen. Then, abruptly, he came to life. Jumping up off the bed, he frantically brushed the white powder off his body. As instructed, he got dressed and located his briefcase and jacket. Then he waited. Minutes later, he entered the black sedan. Murdock, at the wheel, drove them to the research building at the General. It was 3:00 a.m.

"What are we doing here?" Harris asked, confused.

"I want you to get a few things you will need for later."

"Like what?

"Like your DNA liposomes and experimental mice. I'll be waiting right here. If you aren't back in three minutes, I'll call the police with the location of your girlfriend's body. Am I making myself clear?"

Harris got out of the car and walked like a zombie up the stairs to the research building. He swiped his ID across the entry sensor and went inside. The building was deserted. He went to his office and took some vials of his DNA liposomes from the refrigerator, packed them in a container with dry ice, and put it into his satchel briefcase. Next, Harris took his progeria mice in a travel cage and placed it inside his satchel, then walked out to the sedan waiting at the curb.

During the ride, which lasted almost an hour, neither driver nor passenger uttered a word. When the car reached a complex of buildings somewhere in the countryside west of Framingham, it made a turn off the main road. A sign by the entrance had an insignia with DNA helix next it: Celestica.

Murdock led Harris into Building Four, and took the stairs down to a basement corridor. They walked to the room at its end. Murdock unlocked a door and held it open. "This is where you'll be staying, Dr. Harris. The lab has everything necessary you'll need to continue your work. If there is something else you need, just let me know."

Harris entered without objecting. "Goodbye for now," Murdock said, shutting the door. When Harris tried to open it, he found the door locked. Later an armed guard came and led Harris to another room in the same building. The man shoved him into in a chair and tied his arms and legs.

"What's going on?" Harris asked. The guard didn't answer. He merely leaned back against the wall, crossed his arms, and stood silently. A short while later, the man who had driven the black sedan entered the room.

"It's you again?" Harris said.

"Yes, and I hope this won't take long. I know you've had a very stressful night." Harris noticed that the man held something that looked like a truncheon with two metal prongs at one end. "Before I can leave you to settle in, we need to conduct a small business matter. I need you to sign something for me."

"What's that?"

"Just a contract Mr. Anderson gave me. Your signature gives Celestica the rights to the DNA liposomes."

"Don't be ridiculous. I'll never sign that," Harris retorted.

"Hey, read the contract. You get three million bucks. That seems like a pretty good deal to me."

"Forget it. I'm not signing."

"You'll sign anything I want before we're through."

"Are you going to hit me with that thing in your hand?"

"No, this is not for hitting," Murdock answered, holding up the long cylindrical object. "You're a pretty smart guy, so you might appreciate the physics. I call this my magic wand. It causes fifteen thousand volts worth of pain—and no tissue damage. How does that sound?" Harris didn't answer. Murdock continued, "Okay, have it your way. When you ask me nicely, I'll allow you to sign. Now, let's give the magic wand a try."

Murdock touched his power stick to Harris's chest and it discharged with an audible crackle. Harris screamed as his body stiffened from the electrical jolt. The pain was worse than anything he had ever felt in his life. After the forth shock, Harris begged him to stop. Murdock undid one of Harris's arms and allowed him to sign.

10

Flowers and his team entered the apartment where Claire lay dead. Within minutes, everything movable had been taken out and loaded onto a truck parked in the alley—furniture, wall hangings, even carpeting. Claire's body was unceremoniously wrapped in bedding and placed inside the truck with the furniture. Later, her corpse was brought to Building Four at the Celestica complex and thrown into the industrial incinerator. After cremation, only a few ounces of untraceable ash were left of the pretty woman who had earlier seduced Harris.

After finishing his assignment, Flowers strutted into Murdock's office and sat down. "Mission accomplished, boss. The apartment is clean."

"What about the girl?" Murdock asked.

"She went up smokestack of Building Four a little while ago." Flowers pointed at a humidor on the desk. "You mind?"

"Help yourself, Earl. You deserve it." Flowers lit the cigar then took a long, satisfying drag. He blew a thick smoke ring up toward the ceiling.

Murdock smiled, nodding his head in approval. He liked that Flowers never let conscience interfere with a mission.

**

Murdock's security firm, Specialty Security Consultants, charged its clients top dollar for services. The men who worked for him were a closely knit group. Most, like Earl Flowers, had once served under his command. Murdock's platoon had done unspeakable things, all of which they justified as service to their country. Now their work had only one purpose—money. Flowers, like his boss, had a tattoo of a cobra entwining six arrows on his right arm, the insignia of Army Special Forces.

SSC did mainly corporate business. Sometimes its people acted as bodyguards, protecting bigwigs sent to hot spots around the globe. Other times, they recovered important stolen documents or company secrets. For an extra charge, they made sure that those involved got whatever payback their employer requested.

On the surface, the job Jim Anderson offered Murdock didn't seem difficult. The money was good and there was only one man who needed to be brought in. Massachusetts was a hell of a lot safer than other parts of the world where Murdock and his men could get their heads blown off just walking down the street so he accepted. In short order, members of Murdock's SSC team arrived at Celestica's headquarters and assumed control over its small existing security force.

Murdock's plan to frame Harris and hold him in Building Four went without a hitch for several weeks. Then something unexpected happened. Todd, one of the guards from the original Celestica staff, took pity on their prisoner and tried to let him go after a few week of captivity. Harris had been found and brought back in no time, thanks to his embedded tracking chip, but Murdock had no choice but to dispose of the errant guard—and to force Harris to watch. After that, Murdock was certain that Harris would never again try to leave, but the recent breakout proved him wrong.

Murdock called Flowers. "Any progress in locating our doctor?

"We found the company car he stole in a parking lot outside a T station at Boston College. The vehicle was pretty smashed up," said Flowers. "Looks like Harris took the subway. He could've gone anywhere in the city."

"Generate a list of Harris's old friends and associates," said Murdock. "Watch them closely for evidence of contact."

Within twenty-four hours, Flowers had lifted Harris's finger-prints off the doorknob to Chad Reynolds's apartment building. Now Reynolds was under around-the-clock surveillance, with his phone tapped, and computer hacked into.

**

Anderson called his head of security for an update. "So, where is that son of a bitch?"

"I don't know exactly where he is now, but we do know where he's been. We already have evidence he visited an old colleague's apartment," said Murdock. "It's only a matter of time until Harris tries to contact the guy again, and when he does, we'll nab him."

"Damn it, Bill—we don't have time. Witig wants Harris back today, not tomorrow."

How dare that spineless fuck raise his voice at me? Murdock thought. Then he calmed himself. "Look, Jim, if you want to go find him yourself, be my guest."

Anderson exhorted Murdock. "Just…just bring him back alive, and in one piece." Then he hung up.

Murdock had to admit a grudging respect for Harris. The method he had used to escape—burning a hole through solid steel—with thermogenic paste was beyond impressive. And when the signal from the tracking chip disappeared, Murdock knew it could only mean one thing, that Harris had cut it out of his own flesh. Murdock shook his head in acknowledgement of the man he now pursued. *That guy has some real balls for a lab geek doctor.*

11

Chad called Percy Adams, his lab technician assistant. "Percy, I could use your help." "Sure, doc, fire away."

"Three experimental mice arrived by special delivery early this morning. It's important that you start giving them a dose of medication from the vials located in the refrigerator. Each needs to receive one-tenth cc daily."

"That doesn't sound too difficult. What is the stuff I'm giving them?

"It's a gene treatment."

"No sweat, doc. I'll take care of it."

"Just one more thing, when you can."

"What's that?"

"Could you run an analysis on the mice to see if they are related?"

"Sure, I'll have it done by tomorrow."

"Thanks a million, Percy."

After finishing his afternoon clinic, Chad left the hospital and drove to Logan to pick up Kristen. He was anxious to see her, but unsure how much to say about Harris's visit. He spotted her waving at the curbside. Kristen opened the door, put her bag in the back seat, and sat up front. She leaned over to give him a kiss.

During the ride back, Chad was unusually quiet. "Is something wrong?" she asked.

Chad was silent for a moment then spoke. "Kris, remember Dr. Harris?"

"Of course I do. I met him at your departmental Christmas party. Didn't you tell me he left the country for a job abroad?"

"Yes, it was very sudden. He didn't tell anyone he was thinking of leaving, and he never said goodbye...never even cleaned out his office," said Chad. "I hadn't seen or heard from him in over a year."

"And...?"

"And last night around 4:00 a.m. he showed up at the apartment."

"That's odd."

"Wait, it gets even stranger. Harris said he never left the country. He said he's been held prisoner by a pharmaceutical company, forced to do research at a secret lab near Framingham."

"Come on, Chad, you can't be serious." Kristen laughed.

"But I am." The look on his face told her he thought Harris's story was true. "Harris told me this pharmaceutical company, Celestica, tried to buy a drug he discovered—a treatment he'd developed to help children with progeria, a rare disorder that causes premature aging. Most kids with progeria die in adolescence."

"So, the company tried to buy it, and I'm guessing from what you've said that he told them no."

"Correct."

"But why would a company risk keeping him prisoner, especially for a drug used in treatment of such a rare condition?"

"You're right. It doesn't make sense for them to go to such trouble." Chad continued. "But Harris also said they wanted to use his drug not for progeria patients but as a mass market anti-aging treatment for anyone able to afford it."

"Chad, I don't know what to say. Either Harris is off his rocker or he's been victim of a terrible injustice," said Kristen. "If you're asking me, you need to go to the police. Even if you're not asking, I'm telling you that's what you should do."

"I would agree, except Harris specified that there was a reason he *couldn't* go to the authorities yet. Whatever that reason is, I'm going to respect his wishes...at least for now."

"I still think going to the police would be the right thing to do."

Chad turned to her and, changing the subject, said, "You know, I'm really glad you're back, even if you don't agree with me. So, how things are with the folks?"

**

Chad was making rounds at the hospital the next morning when his pager went off. It was Percy, over at the research facility.

"Say, doc, it's about those mice. I did the DNA analysis, and it's the strangest thing. The female, the youngest looking one of the bunch, she's actually the mother of the two males. I can't figure it out for the life of me."

"Are you absolutely sure?"

"Well, the males have the same mitochondrial DNA as the female, so they're all related. They also have serial numbers tattooed on their bellies. I found those numbers in our database. The mice are originally from our facility, and the female's date of birth was eight months earlier than the males'—and they're listed in the log as her offspring. She's their mother, for sure, no doubt about it. But she *looks* so much younger. I just don't freakin' understand."

Chad felt a chill run down his spine. What Harris had told him about the mice was confirmed. It defied conventional wisdom, but indicated that Harris's story was true. "Percy, can I ask one more favor? Can you keep this between us?"

"Sure, doc, it stays between you and me, no one else."

Chad hung up and returned to rounds with his team, but his mind was elsewhere. He tried to focus as the residents presented their cases, but he was still thinking about Harris and his mystery mice. After rounds, he sat at his office computer and checked his e-mail. Among the many addresses that popped up in his in-box, one stuck out since he hadn't seen it in a long time—genedoc@ BG.org—Harris's old e-mail address at Boston General.

The General had one of the most secure computer systems anywhere. Some on the staff joked that it was probably easier to hack into the Pentagon computers than to get into the hospital network, and they were probably correct. The hospital had sponsored an ongoing MIT competition to test the information system's security, offering a thousand dollars to any student who could penetrate the system. As yet, there had been no winners.

Chad clicked on the message.

Chad,

It's too risky for me to contact you by phone or on your home computer. Celestica is probably monitoring your communications and we need to be careful. Since officially I am on an extended leave of absence, my access to the hospital e-mail is still active. It gives me a secure way to contact you and explain a few things.

I couldn't let Celestica get away with their plans for my DNA liposomes. Although the treatment slows aging, there is one very serious side effect. Stopping the treatment suddenly leads to fatal hyperthermia. It's far too dangerous a treatment to be used by anyone who isn't closely monitored or doesn't already have a life-threatening disorder like progeria.

I am using a computer at an Internet café not far from where I'm staying. I will e-mail you back to let you know where and when we can meet. If anything should happen that results in my death, please do what you can to see that my DNA liposomes are used only for their intended purpose, treating children with progeria. The formula with instructions on how to produce the liposomes is on the disk I left you. Thank God you agreed to help me.

—Gordon

Chad stared at the computer screen. He had to help his friend, Gordon. But how?

12

olfield felt queasy from the helicopter ride. He was heading to a meeting with Gustav Jung, the CEO of Novara, who was cruising on his yacht a few nautical miles south of Nice. The chopper landed on a pad at the yacht's stern just before motion sickness got the best of him.

Awaiting his guest's arrival, Jung stood just off the helipad. Should his rival's newest drug prospect, Juvena, be denied approval as Holfield suggested it would be, Celestica's stock price would go into a free-fall. Jung would then be able to buy Witig's company for next to nothing. Unlike Witig, who was heir to Celestica, Jung had worked his way up the corporate ladder the hard way. To him, Witig was nothing more than a spoiled brat who had inherited a great company that he was slowly running into the ground. Jung was certain he could do a better job.

Exiting the helicopter, Holfield ducked under the still-rotating blades and walked over to shake Jung's outstretched hand. "Come," Jung beckoned. "Let's have some lunch. Afterward, we can talk business."

On the lower deck, Jung's chef had prepared a sumptuous buffet. They sat outside, eating a first course of caviar and pâté, surrounded by the glistening waters of the Mediterranean. When lunch was over, Jung offered Holfield a cognac. As they sat and sipped their drinks, Jung said, "Well, let's see what you've got."

"I thought our arrangement was that you would show me the money first."

"As you like," Jung said. He reached under the table and produced a metal briefcase. Jung made a space, then placed the case on the table and opened its combination lock. It was filled with money. "Five hundred thousand in cash as agreed upon. The balance will be wired to your account in Zurich, provided you give me proof of your assertions."

Holfield eyed the cash with delight. "Gustav, you are a man of your word."

"Now, please. I'd like your information about Juvena."

Holfield began. "First, let me say that the injections work. Juvena slows the aging process substantially. But the better news, from *your* standpoint, is that if the treatment is stopped abruptly, it causes certain death. And the death is not a pleasant one. Malignant hyperthermia develops, with seizures and hemorrhaging."

Jung smiled contentedly. "Yes, that *is* good news—very good news."

"Witig plans on keeping this complication secret from the EU regulatory agency. He is absolutely desperate to get Juvena approved as soon as possible. After that, he plans to tell the agency about the complication and propose that a black-box warning be added to the label. The warning would direct that the injections be slowly withdrawn rather than stopped abruptly. Our lead scientist, the man who discovered Juvena, found that this approach avoids the hyperthermic reaction."

Holfield pulled a file from his briefcase. "Here's the proof you asked for."

Jung opened the file and laid it on top of the money in the briefcase as Holfield explained its contents. "These are the two subjects who died in our clinical trial and their autopsy findings."

Jung examined the pictures of the dead subjects, their bodies covered with ugly bruises. "This is wonderful," Jung said gleaming. "These photos will put the last nail in Witig's corporate coffin."

"I was certain you would be pleased, Herr Jung."

Jung poured them each a glass of champagne. Toasting his guest, he said, "I congratulate you on your foresight in coming forward with this information." He sipped his drink. "I will see to it that an acquaintance of mine on the regulatory agency is appraised of the situation." Jung patted Holfield on the back. "Unfortunately, I must end our discussions for the moment. I am expected back in Bern tonight. However, if you like, my yacht and crew are at your disposal for the weekend. A little respite from the savannas of Africa seems in order. What say you?"

"That is most kind, Herr Jung."

"And something else. It would make me happy if you joined my team at Novara," said Jung. "Then you can say farewell to Africa and Witig forever."

"Yes," Holfield said with a broad grin. "That would be marvelous."

Jung embraced Paul Holfield like an old friend then walked away, carrying the file. Minutes later, the helicopter took off. In a matter of hours Jung, would be back at Novara headquarters in Switzerland with the evidence he needed to crush his competitor.

**

Holfield had tired of life in Kinshasa. The gambling there was mediocre, and the women were a constant worry because of rampant AIDS. Thankfully, with a new face constructed by skilled plastic surgeons in Costa Rica, and a new identity as the Canadian, Paul Holfield, he remained a free man. Interpol was still looking for George Fleming, convicted *in absentia* of illegal human experimentation and murder in Mexico, but they would never find him.

Holfield had learned well from his Mexican misadventure. He would never again remain on a sinking ship. His departure from the Jamison Institute just before the authorities descended on the facility had been much too close for comfort. Holfield could see the writing on the wall for Celestica Pharmaceutical, and was ready to bail. The drug worked: Juvena slowed aging. But once it was known that it had caused two deaths in subjects who had stopped using the drug suddenly, and with more fatalities possibly in the offing, there was no hope of getting it approved by the European Medicines Agency, let alone the USFDA. Holfield had entertained the idea of contacting Witig's rival, Gustav Jung, following the first research subject's death. After the second one died, he set up a clandestine meeting to transfer the evidence—and his loyalties.

Now, with the deal consummated, Holfield was intent on celebrating. As soon as his host departed, Holfield phoned to make arrangements for his evening activities. After dinner, a crew member ferried Holfield to the harbor in Monte Carlo, where a waiting limousine drove him from the dock to the casino. At 2:00 a.m., he returned to the yacht. He'd had too much to drink and had trouble walking, but fortunately Monique and Monika were happy to assist. Holfield had made arrangement for the two party girls to be waiting for him in his limo when he finished at the Casino de Paris. On the jetty ride back they helped steady him and made sure their wealthy benefactor didn't fall overboard

Holfield staggered down the passageway of the yacht on his way to the master bedroom, with his girlfriends holding him up. He fell onto the large circular bed; the women followed. In short order, they had undressed themselves and their host. Both had beautiful bodies, but Monika's was more muscular and she had gold posts piercing her nipples.

Monique's head bobbed up and down as she gave Holfield oral sex. Meanwhile, Monika opened the backpack she had brought along then donned a skintight black leather outfit that left her privates and pierced nipples exposed. She took a tube of lubricant and a vibrator then climbed onto the bed. While Monique continued attending to Holfield, Monika rubbed some lubricant on the vibrator's tip and inserted it into her partner from behind as Holfield watched in delight. Finally, Monika slapped her partner's backside and exclaimed, "Enough of that you bitch. Get on your back!"

Monique stopped working on Holfield and did as ordered. She spread her legs and was soon moaning with pleasure as Monika again used the vibrator on her. Holfield looked on, his desire building.

Finally, he blurted out, "I can do better than that silly battery-operated toy!" He pushed Monika out of the way, flipped Monique over, and entered her. Unperturbed, Monika went back to her bag and took out a whip. She gently stroked its flanges across his back as Holfield moved back and forth over Monique, grunting in utter sexual abandon.

She bent down and whispered into his ear, "Monika hears you've been a bad boy...a very bad boy." She hit him with the whip, raising lines of red welt across his back. A moment later, she hit him once again, harder. Holfield was beside himself in ecstasy. It was exactly what he was looking for. His night on Jung's yacht was off to a good start.

13

Jim Anderson had accepted the position as manager of Celestica's American division for Rolfe Witig's offer of top salary plus stock options. Now his financial future was in dire jeopardy. The company pipeline was nearly empty of promise, except for Juvena. Everything rested on its success.

The plan to kidnap and hold Harris was his and Anderson had received Witig's fervent blessing. Up until Harris's escape, Murdock had executed the mission with perfection. However, now they were in a race against time. Anderson needed Harris back to finish work essential for regulatory approval. Sitting in his office, Anderson had the unsettling vision of his stock option certificates being used for wallpaper. He needed to calm his frayed nerves. He uncapped the bottle of Johnny Walker from his desk and poured a stiff drink, then closed his eyes and sighed with relief as the whiskey went down. *Why worry? With Murdock after him, Harris hasn't got a chance.*

✳✳

Chad's pager went off at the hospital and an unfamiliar number appeared on its screen. He dialed the number. He did not recognize the voice that answered.

"Dr. Reynolds? My name is Dr. Harold Sumner. I understand you are a friend of Dr. Gordon Harris."

"That's correct," Chad answered.

"Well, I cared for Dr. Harris after his breakdown. He was undergoing psychiatric treatment at our private facility until he ran away several days ago. We've been trying to locate him ever since." Sumner paused for a moment. "I need to alert you that Harris suffers from paranoid schizophrenia and could be a danger to himself or others. I am checking with anyone who may have had contact with him to let them know. As you might imagine, the hospitalization was very hush-hush, to protect his reputation."

Then Sumner pointedly asked, "Dr. Reynolds, have you heard from Harris?"

Chad thought quickly. If Harris was really schizophrenic, he certainly needed treatment. But what if Sumner was a phony? Chad decided to give Harris the benefit of the doubt. "I'm sorry about Dr. Harris's illness. But no, I haven't heard a thing. Why don't you give me a number where I can reach you if I do hear from him?"

On the other end of the line, Earl Flowers said, "Call my personal cell, any time of the day or night, if you find out anything that can help." He recited a number.

"Of course, Dr. Sumner, I will. You can count on it."

Flowers later reported to Murdock, "Reynolds didn't fall for the story."

"Unfortunately, the bastard is too clever for his own good. I think he knows something— in fact, he knows too much. Once we've got Harris back, Reynolds and that live in girlfriend of his will have to be eliminated."

**

Kristen made dinner that evening. She had enjoyed the brief visit with her parents, but was glad to be back in Boston. "Have you heard any more from Gordon?" she asked, over dinner.

Chad turned the music up just in case the apartment was bugged and mimed Kristen to speak softly.

"Yes, an e-mail through the General's network. Gordon is in hiding."

"Will you see him again?"

"I'm waiting to hear from him. In the meantime, I had a disturbing call from a man who claimed Gordon is unstable."

"What do you mean?" Kristen asked.

"A man named Sumner claimed to be Gordon's psychiatrist. He said Harris suffers from paranoid schizophrenia, and ran away for the facility where he was being treated."

"Did you tell him Gordon came to our apartment?"

"No. The whole thing sounded fishy to me," said Chad. "I still believe Gordon's story. I don't want to, but I do."

"You're not in danger, are you?" Kristen asked with a worried look on her face.

"I don't think so," Chad answered. But secretly, he felt far from safe.

**

In the morning, Percy entered Chad's office in the research building with a baffled look.. "Dr. Reynolds, can I interrupt you?" he asked.

"Sure, Percy, what's up?"

"Well, I'll tell you what's up. It's those three mice. I can't stop thinking about them. It's just too weird. You've got to tell me—" Percy stopped in midsentence. "Wait, are you testing me, checking to see if I know my stuff? Is this some joke? What's really going on?"

"Percy, I've known you for a long time, and you've known me. I wouldn't lie to you. I can't tell you the whole story yet, but I can say the mice are no joke. It has something to do with Dr. Harris's research on progeria. I hope for now you'll bear with me, and keep this a secret."

"All right, I can manage that. But I need you to explain as soon as possible, because it's driving me nuts."

"I absolutely promise, I will." Chad answered, leaving his technician temporarily satisfied. After he left the office, Chad popped Harris's Juvena project disk into his computer. Multiple files appeared. He opened the first.

Chad,

If you are reading this, then you have agreed to help me under what you know by now are difficult and dangerous circumstances. I thank you in advance from the bottom of my heart.

Let me give you a little background on the DNA liposomes treatment for progeria. A few years ago, one of my progeria patients died. Seth was twelve and looked every bit of eighty. I had been seeing him in the clinic for several years. While attending his funeral service I noticed a boy sitting between Seth's father and mother. For a moment I thought was looking at Seth had he been alive and a normal child. He was twelve, too—and turned out to be his brother's identical twin. Then it dawned on me what I needed to do to solve the problem of progeria. At birth, both children were totally identical. It was only as they got older that Seth's accelerated aging caused them to look radically different. I knew that as identical twin, Seth and his brother had begun with exactly the same DNA, with one exception—the mutation in Seth's which caused progeria. His parents were kind enough to allow me to take an oral swab for analysis. By comparing Seth's DNA with that of his brother, I pinpointed the gene defect responsible for progeria.

The abnormality was on chromosome twenty-one, the smallest of all the chromosomes, but certainly not the least important. The mutation was in a promoter sequence that serves to activate multiple genes, all involved in aging. You will find more detailed information in the other files on this CD.

Chad, I value your friendship. I wish I did not have to enlist you in this dangerous business, but I need an ally I can trust. Take good care,

—Gordon

Chad felt an odd sense of relief after reading the message. It was now absolutely clear to him that everything Harris had told him was true. He had never left Boston General to take a job overseas. He had never lost his mind. Harris had been kidnapped... for his *research*—including the information on this disk.

Chad scanned through the other files. They contained in-depth information about the normal and abnormal gene located on chromosome twenty-one. By delivering the normal DNA sequence of the promoter gene packaged inside a liposome, Harris had been able to radically slow the accelerated aging process in his mouse model for progeria. The data he included on the disk showed that the levels of free radicals in their tissue and blood dropped dramatically with treatment, indicating a slowing of cellular aging. Telomere length remained unchanged or even increased. Harris had even begun testing his DNA liposomes in primates. The stage was being set for human trials.

Chad was transfixed by the information he reviewed. Harris had not only discovered how the human biological clock works, but had found a way to slow it down. He'd done it thanks to the brother of his patient who died from a rare, fatal disease of premature aging, progeria.

Chad understood that Harris had made a landmark discovery in understanding aging, one that could potentially help all patients afflicted with progeria.

That is, once he was free of the murderous thugs who were chasing him. Chad had to find a way to help.

14

Todd was lying on a concrete floor with his hands and feet bound, duct tape plastered over his mouth. Harris sat in a chair facing him, his own arms and legs tied so he couldn't move. His eyes were taped open so he had no choice but to watch.

The industrial incinerator in Building Four burned at two thousand degrees, its high temperature required to convert biological materials, like the animals spent in experiments, into carbon dust. Murdock walked over to Todd and kicked him hard in the side. The duct tape barely muffled Todd's agonized groan.

Murdock screamed down at the young guard, "You pathetic piece of shit! I paid you to work for me, not for Harris. What the hell did you think you were doing, leaving his door unlocked?"

Murdock headed toward the incinerator and pulled a lever, opening its heavy metal cover. Harris felt a blast of heat hit his face. "Let's get this over with quick," Murdock said to the security men accompanying him. "Throw the son of a bitch in."

Harris was in shock as he watched the horrific event unfold. The guards lifted Todd. "No! Stop! You can't do this!" Harris shouted, but his words had no effect. Todd's thrashing body disappeared into the inferno. Murdock released the lever and the cover shut with a resounding bang.

Harris felt ill. He had just witnessed something positively medieval in its barbarity. His body shook uncontrollably. Murdock walked over and yanked Harris by the hair so he looked directly into his face. Glaring menacingly, Murdock said, "You'll be next, doctor, if you ever try to pull any more funny stuff. I may not be a fucking PhD, but don't take me for a fool. You do your research and stay put in the lab, or you'll end up in the incinerator like our friend."

Harris awoke in a sweat, his heart pounding. It was the same dream he'd had a half dozen times before. But the first time, it had been no dream. Following his first aborted escape, the events had played out exactly that way in real life, down to the last detail. Now, as he relived the experience during sleep, he could still hear Todd's stifled screams and the clang of the incinerator door shutting.

The company's heartless, pointless murder of the sympathetic guard made Harris all the more determined to prevent Celestica from stealing his discovery. Todd had died for trying to help him; he could not let that death go unanswered. He had Claire's death to avenge as well.

Harris ventured out of the boardinghouse in Cambridge only when necessary. He made his trips as brief as possible. At least he had figured out a safe way to communicate with Chad using the secure Boston General e-mail. Finally, he hatched a plan.

**

After clinic, Chad checked his hospital computer. A one sentence e-mail message had arrived from Harris:

> *Meet me tomorrow morning inside Faneuil Hall at 9 a.m. and be careful that no one follows. Gordon*

The next morning was Saturday. Chad got up while Kristen still slept. He left the apartment building and stretched before his run, casually looking to see if there was anyone suspicious around, then took off. After running about two miles, he abruptly crossed the street and slipped into a T station entrance. He took two different trains, and got off at Boston Common. In another few minutes, he arrived at Faneuil Hall. Before entering, he stopped and bent down with his hands on his knees, pretending to regain his wind while he surveyed the area. Then he went inside. A minute later, he saw Harris coming down an aisle toward him. This time, Harris looked clean-shaven, like the man Chad remembered. He reached out to shake Chad's hand, but once he took it didn't let go. Instead, he pulled him toward an exit.

"Thanks for coming," Harris said. "Let's grab a bite to eat across the way and chat. There's much to talk about." They exited the building and headed to a crowded café.

Harris began, "I didn't have time to tell you before, but there is an important reason I couldn't go to the police. I was set up by Celestica. They staged everything...and now they have blackmail photos that make me look like a murderer, or at least like a drug user guilty of manslaughter." He told Chad the whole sordid story. "Now you can see why I can't go straight to the police."

Chad shook his head and exclaimed, "Holy Christ!"

Harris took a sip of coffee. "I was still muddled from the alcohol and the sedative, so when the phone in the apartment rang and the man told me it would all go away if I followed his instructions, like a fool I complied. I didn't even know it was about my research until they had me in their clutches. And they wouldn't let go."

"You know for sure it was Celestica?"

"I was held at the Celestica facility, in a basement lab. I saw Jim Anderson, the man I went to seeking funding, and I signed...they forced me to sign documents that will make it look as though I willingly sold my research to Celestica."

The two ate in silence for a moment. "Jeez, Gordon. I know Big Pharma has power and controls billions, but I never thought..." Chad's voice trailed away.

"Yes, I know. It's a nightmare," said Harris. "The rough stuff Celestica does is all handled by an ex-military man named Murdock. He and his band of thugs are more like mercenaries than security. As we sit here now having this nice breakfast, I'm sure he's got his jackals running around the city hunting for me."

"Gordon, you're a respected scientist. Don't you think the police would believe you if you went to them with this story? I mean, you've got the mice, and—"

"No. Even if I prepared them for the memory chip of incriminating pictures that Murdock would no doubt send, the investigation would be enough to ruin me...at least long enough for Celestica to find some way to make millions off Juvena and possibly hurt others in the process. I can't be locked up while this drags through the courts. These people are ruthless."

"True. Kidnapping you, killing a woman—that's way beyond business as usual," Chad said.

Harris went on, "Claire wasn't the only one they murdered. I tried escaping before, fairly soon after I was taken. One of the original Celestica security guards, a young kid, not one of Murdock's 'special hires,' felt bad for me and left my door unlocked. Murdock had him thrown into an incinerator right in front of me. After that, I vowed that I would get out—and take my discovery with me."

"The people who did this to you are insane!" Chad blurted out.

"There's another important reason that Celestica must *never* be allowed get the DNA liposomes to market."

"What's that?" Chad asked. "I thought you said it worked?"

"It does work. But if the injections are stopped abruptly in lab mice, the mice invariably die of a severe hyperthermic reaction. It would be no different for humans. A sudden profound activation of their dormant cellular oxidizing systems occurs. In spite of that knowledge, Celestica is going ahead with plans for drug distribution. Juvena must only be used to treat those afflicted with progeria. It's much too risky for the widespread public use they intend."

"What can we do?" Chad asked.

"Well, for one thing, I have to get the chip they're using to blackmail me."

"They probably have copies."

"True, but I have something else in mind. Once I have it, I'll take it to the police myself."

"Aren't you worried they'll charge you with the crime you didn't commit?"

"How many killers voluntarily take evidence of their crime and turn it in?"

"Not many."

"Murdock and Celestica murdered an innocent woman and a kid who tried to help me. Now they are depriving a life-saving treatment for patients with progeria and could end up killing scores of others whose only fault is they want to stay young. I cannot let that happen."

"What can I do?"

"Well, Celestica wants my mice to use as a demonstration of the DNA liposome effect for the regulatory panel. What if you act as the middleman and propose a trade—the mice for the memory chip?" Harris held up his hand at Chad's shocked look. "I'm sure they would be more than happy to part with a chip they have copies of. But we'll one-up them."

"And how is that?"

"You'll give them three similar but different mice, and we'll keep the ones I gave you. It should take a couple days for them to do the DNA analysis and realize what happened, giving me enough time to go to the police."

They spent the next hour talking through the details. Before they parted, Chad gave Harris his hospital pager. "Here, take this. I'll get another. We can use it to stay in touch without having to use a computer. You can type messages directly into it."

Harris took the pager and headed back to Cambridge.

**

When he returned home, Chad phoned the number for Harris's supposed psychiatrist. Flowers answered the call.

"Dr. Sumner, or whatever your real name is, I'd like to propose a deal."

"I'm sorry, I don't understand."

"Look, you're no psychiatrist, so cut the charade. I've heard from Dr. Harris, and he asked me to relay a message to you. I don't know what it means, but he said he's willing to give you the mice if you give him the chip with the pictures, and promise to leave him alone."

"That's the whole message?"

"That's the message."

"Can I speak with Dr. Harris myself? I'd like to ask him some questions."

"It's not possible. And he said he wants an answer within the next twenty-four hours or he will stop injecting the mice and let them die."

"I see," Flowers mumbled.

"Within twenty-four hours, or else." Chad hung up.

15

Flowers phoned Murdock. "Reynolds wants to exchange the mice for our memory chip and your word that we'll leave Harris alone."

"That asshole Reynolds is just making things more difficult," Murdock said, his voice rising. "He's going out of his way to help Harris and try to fuck us over."

"What do you think we should do?" Flowers asked.

"Go ahead and arrange an exchange," Murdock answered. "Take the chip and try to be as friendly as possible. Assure Reynolds we'll forget about Harris if he gives us the research mice. Anderson is hot to get them back as soon as possible since Witig needs the mice for a demonstration with the European regulatory agency." Murdock slammed his palm on the desk and grinned. "Ha! I'll bet that soon after the exchange, Reynolds and Harris will meet to celebrate. That's when we'll get them both."

**

Chad went to his lab in the research building and found Percy. "How are the mice doing?" he asked.

"So far they're acting like the thousand other rodents in this building. They haven't stood up on their hind legs and started singing, if that's what you're wondering."

Chad chuckled. "Percy, I need another favor."

"Like…what?"

"Can you find three other mice that match the color, size, and sex of those three?"

"You're not planning anything that could get us in trouble, are you? You're not asking me to fake research or anything like that?"

"No, I promise, I am not doing anything even remotely unethical." Chad continued. "It's very, very important…but very, very confidential. Soon I should be able to explain the whole thing to you, but right now, I need this big favor."

"You'll tell me how it is that the mother seems younger than her children? And if there's a paper to publish in this, you'll mention my name in the credits?"

"Yes, I'll tell you everything. And put you on the paper."

"Then I'll have your three new mice by late this afternoon. I'm sure I can find some decent matches. You want the serial numbers tattooed on their bellies to be the same, I assume?"

"Yes, the serial numbers *have* to match, and Percy, thanks a million. You have no idea how much this means."

✱✱

Chad was making rounds when his beeper went off. The message he received from Harris was brief:

"Do we have a deal?"

Chad typed back. *"I'm not sure. The offer is in, but they haven't responded yet."*

"Were you able to get substitute mice?"

"It's in the works."

"Chad, don't forget—we're dealing with dangerous men. They kill people who get in the way."

"I understand and I'll be careful." Chad added, *"I'll page you after the exchange takes place."*

His return message, *"Good luck my friend."*

Chad typed in a final correspondence. *"Thanks, I'll need it."*

**

Anderson phoned Witig. "We have a more serious problem than I originally thought. Harris took the mice we were going to use for your demonstration."

"Shit!" Witig screamed into the phone.

Anderson tried to defuse his irate boss. "Murdock assures me that we'll have Harris—*and* his mice—back shortly."

"Just be quick about it," Witig barked. Then he said, in a calmer tone, "Offer him an extra hundred thousand if he gets it done in forty-eight hours."

Anderson phoned Murdock. "There's a little bonus for you if you get Harris and his mice back within the next forty-eight hours."

"How much are we talking about?"

"Does one hundred thousand sound good?"

"That's a decent piece of change. Let me thank you in advance."

Hanging up his phone, Murdock began thinking about how he would spend the bonus he intended to collect.

16

C had answered his phone and heard the voice of Harris's phony psychiatrist. "You've got a deal. Bring me the mice, and I'll give you the chip."

"And you promise to leave Dr. Harris alone?"

"Sure, that too, but first you have to give me the mice."

"Okay, meet me at Boston Common by the entrance to the swan ride, tomorrow morning at eleven." Chad and Harris had decided during their meeting that the Common, one of the most public places in Boston, would be a relatively safe spot to consummate a deal with dangerous men. There would certainly be less chance for foul play in plain view of everyone in the park.

"I'll be there." Earl Flowers answered.

"How will I find you?"

"Don't worry Dr. Reynolds. I know exactly what you look like."

From a phone in the hospital lobby, Chad called Percy at the research building. "Do you have them?"

"Yes, I have your mice body-doubles ready. They look just like the ones you gave me. I tattooed the same numerals on their underbellies, so the critters are ready and waiting for you."

Chad hung up. So far the plan was developing just the way he and Harris had intended. The next morning, Chad stopped by his lab and picked up the counterfeit mice. Percy was absolutely right; they were indistinguishable from the progeria mice Harris had given him. Chad placed their small enclosure in a shopping bag and marched off for the Common.

Flowers sat on a bench close to the swan ride, feeding popcorn to pigeons. One of his men was stationed nearby to track Reynolds's movements once the exchange was made.

Chad entered the park. He was nervous and held the shopping bag with its mice inside tightly under his arm. Flowers spotted him, got up from the bench then approached Chad from behind. "Dr. Reynolds."

Chad recognized the voice and turned around.

Flowers said, "It's quite noble of you to help your friend Harris."

"Look, save your sarcasm. Harris and I want nothing more to do with you or anyone one else who works for Celestica once our business here is over."

"That's fine with me," said Flowers. "Did you bring the mice, as we discussed?"

Chad nodded his head in affirmation and tapped the shopping bag under his arm. "They are in here. And you have the picture chip?"

"Yes, of course," Flowers answered. "I have it." He reached into his pocket and held out a memory chip for Chad to see.

"Now, may I see the mice?"

Chad opened the shopping bag and displayed the cage inside. Flowers looked them over, checking their serial numbers against those written on a piece of paper and noted. "Things seem to be in order."

"How do I know this chip is the one with the pictures of Harris?" Chad asked.

"Well, I guess you'll just have to take my word for it."

"I don't think so." Chad retorted, leaving no doubt about his firm determination.

Flowers was losing his patience, but tried to control his emotion. Chad pointed to an electronics store across the street. "Let's go over there," he suggested. "I'm sure they have a camera in the shop I can use to check your photo chip."

"Sure. That will work. But let me warn you, there's some pretty nasty stuff on it."

They made their way through traffic crossing the street and entered the store. Chad located a floor model in the camera section and popped the memory chip into it. The camera's display screen lit up. In the first picture, he could make out Harris, naked, on a bed with a woman sprawled next to him. The next image showed the woman lying on top of Harris, like they were having sex. Another showed Harris with his head between her legs. The final picture showed a syringe in the woman's arm with a loosened tourniquet above. Chad had seen enough.

He knew the photos had been staged while Harris was in a stupor and the woman was dead, but Chad had to turn his head away. He was sickened by the images. Chad needed to clear his head. Leaving the camera he grabbed his bag and walked out of the store. Outside, Chad leaned against a wall and took a few deep breaths. *Pull yourself together.*

Moments later, Flowers emerged from the store. "The chip you wanted so badly?" he said, extending his hand. "You left it in the camera."

Chad took it as Flowers told him, "And now if you please, give me what I came for." He handed over the bag with his mice. "Thank you, Dr. Reynolds. I hope we *never* have reason to see each other again."

"Likewise," Chad said. Each headed off in a different direction. Chad was glad the exchange was over, but he wasn't in a celebratory mood. The photos he had viewed showed a man he revered as the world's authority on genetics, naked in bed with a woman dead of a drug overdose. It revolted him to think about the extent to which Celestica would go to set Harris up like that. Chad sincerely doubted he could trust the words spoken by the man he had just made a deal with. The very thought of crossing paths with him again sent a chill down his spine.

**

When he arrived home, Kristen immediately noticed Chad looked pale and asked, "Honey, what happened? Are you ill?"

"I'm not feeling all that well right now, but at least I got the memory chip Gordon needs." Chad pulled it from his pocket and held the chip up for her to see with a half-smile.

Kristen said, "I'm sure he'll be very happy to hear you have it."

"Yes. And I promised to let him know right away." Chad sat down at the desk and sent an alphanumeric message for Harris on his pager.

I've got the chip. Everything went smoothly. Where can we meet?

Chad forced himself to start eating the dinner Kristen had prepared, but he had no appetite. A minute later, his hospital pager went off. Chad expected it to be Harris. He pushed his plate away and picked up the pager. The number surprised him. It was his lab. He called immediately.

Percy answered. "Dr. Reynolds, you need to come to the lab pronto." Chad heard the concern in his voice.

"What's wrong?"

"Look, I need you here...now." Percy hung up. It was seven-thirty in the evening.

Chad told Kristen, "There's some kind of emergency over at the research lab." He looked down at his uneaten food. "I'm not that hungry anyway. Do me a favor and stick this in the fridge; I'll eat it when I get back."

He rushed out and drove quickly to the Boston General Research Building. Percy wasn't someone who would easily wilt in a difficult situation. If he called Chad for help, something very serious must be wrong. Chad ran up the stairs toward his lab, heart pounding. Percy was inside, looking worried. "What's up?" Chad asked, breathless.

"Come on, I'll show you." Chad followed Percy out of the lab and down the hall toward the room that housed most of the unit's experimental animals—mice, rabbits, dogs, and monkeys—used in myriad research projects in the building. A din of barking and screeching greeted them. Percy marched to a treatment table used for veterinary care and pointed toward the Plexiglas enclosure sitting on the table under an examination light. "It's those miracle mice you brought me, the real ones. They started acting a little strange yesterday and today, when I came in, I found this."

Chad saw the mother mouse lying on her side, hyperventilating. Her offspring were on their sides, trying to stand then falling over. Percy said, "They have fevers, and as you can see, this weird behavior. I sent blood for analysis. The results show a normal white blood cell count, so this probably isn't an infection. I can't explain it, but there's no doubt these mice are pretty sick and getting worse."

Chad had to agree.

"Shall I have the vet make an emergency visit?" Percy asked.

"Not yet." Chad wasn't sure he wanted to involve anyone else in the secret of Harris's mice. Just then his pager went off, and he looked down at the display. It was Harris. Chad dialed the number on the hospital phone.

"You got the chip?"

"Yes, things went pretty smoothly."

"Did you see what was on it?"

"Most of it."

"Was it bad?"

"It was pretty awful, but right now we have a more urgent problem. Your mice are sick. They're on their sides, hyperventilating. They can't stand. The white cell count isn't elevated, but they have fevers. The mother looks even worse than her children. She's not even trying to stand anymore. I have no idea what's going on. What do you think it is?"

"Who's been caring for them?" Harris asked.

"Percy Adams, the lab tech. He's been giving the mice their daily dose of your DNA liposomes."

"Sure I remember Percy. He's terrific," said Harris. "Is he there? Can I speak to him?"

Chad handed the phone to Percy, saying, "Dr. Harris needs to speak with you."

"Percy, this is Gordon Harris. How are you?"

"Dr. Harris! It's good to hear your voice again. We miss you around here," said Percy. "You know, I had a feeling you had something to do with these miracle mice. I'm sorry to say, they're sick as hell."

"Percy, have you been administering the substance from the vials Chad gave you?"

"Yes, every day. I put one-tenth cc in their feed, just as I was told."

"I see." Harris said. Then he continued. "Percy, thank you. Now can you put Dr. Reynolds back on the phone for me?"

Percy handed the phone to Chad.

"Gordon?"

"I think I know what the problem is. The mice have been getting the liposomes in their diet instead of by direct injection. When it is taken orally, the liposomes get digested in the stomach. So the mice have not been getting any of it into their systems. They're showing the first signs of a hyperthermic reaction that could be fatal."

"Dammit—that's my mistake," said Chad. "I'm sorry! I don't think I specified that the dose had to be given by injection, not by mouth. Do you think we can save them?"

"I'm not sure, but why don't you try this: give them a double-dose by injection right away, then a single dose every three hours for the next twenty-four. We'll see what happens." Harris was silent for a moment. "Now you can see one of the main reasons I don't want my DNA liposomes available to the general public. Patients forget things, they're noncompliant, and the substance can degrade if left unrefrigerated...I have no doubt that many innocent people would end up having lethal hyperthermia."

"Didn't Celestica realize how serious the problem this could be?" Chad asked.

"I'm afraid they not only knew about it, but in their own twisted way saw it as an advantage. People who started taking Juvena injections would have to take them for the rest of their extended life spans. It was a financial dream come true—getting people hooked forever on an expensive treatment to stay young."

"It's mind-boggling to think that persons running a major pharmaceutical company would put profit above simple human decency."

Harris chided cynically. "Is it? Well, those are the kind of people I've had to contend with over the last year."

"Percy and I will get working on the mice right away."

"Let me know about their progress and remember to be very careful. Celestica is still a threat. I'm not sure what they'll do once they discover that they don't have the real progeria mice, but I doubt they'll just let it drop."

Chad hung up and turned to Percy. "This is all my fault. Unfortunately, when I asked you to give the mice their daily dose, I didn't tell you that it had to be administered by injection." Chad continued. "The mice are undergoing a withdrawal reaction. I'm afraid we've got some hard work ahead of us. Dr. Harris suggests that the mice need a double dose of the substance now, and a regular injection every three hours around the clock. Even with that, they may not make it."

"Is there anything else we can do?"

"We need to find a safe way of cooling the mice down. They're experiencing hyperthermia."

"I don't have anything here, but couldn't we get one of those portable cooling units used at the hospital? I think I could rig it up for our three tiny patients."

"Percy, you're brilliant!"

"Thanks, boss. Maybe you'll consider that the next time I come up for a raise."

Chad's lab tech ran over to the hospital and took a cooling blanket from the storeroom. He placed it under the cage so the temperature inside dropped. For the rest of the night, they took turns tending to the sick mice, giving them their injections. By dawn, the mice were still alive, and seemed to be improved. The mother began taking food and water. Her offspring were able to stand without falling over. Chad and Percy, exhausted after the night up, had renewed optimism for their recovery.

17

Flowers reported to Murdock, "The exchange went without a hitch."

"That's good."

"Of course, the smartass wanted to see what was on the chip, so I let him look." Flowers chortled, "I don't think he was so thrilled by what he saw. He turned white as a ghost. I thought he was going to pass out."

"Serves the son of a bitch right," Murdock said, smirking.

"I had Reynolds followed. From the Common, he went straight to his apartment. Then after dinner, he went to the research building at Boston General. There was no sign of contact with Harris."

"Well, Reynolds may be a workaholic physician, but he's also working hard at being a big pain in the ass to us," said Murdock.

After being up all night, Chad was exhausted but pleased that the mice seemed to be on a road to recovery. It was 6:00 a.m. and Kristen was just getting up when Chad walked in the door.

"What happened?" she asked. "I fell asleep reading. I was surprised when I got up this morning to see that you still hadn't come home."

"The emergency was Harris's experimental mice. They got sick, and we thought they might die. Luckily, Percy and I were able to pull them through during the night. This morning they're looking much better." Chad took out the pager. "I promised to give Harris an update. He wanted to know how things are going." Chad typed in a message:

Suggestions worked. Mice are much better. We need meeting place to hand off the memory chip.

Chad quickly showered, dressed, and ate a little breakfast. "I should be back around dinner time," he told Kristen.

"Well, have a good day," she said back, but Chad was already out the door before she finished her sentence.

While rounding with his team, Chad's pager went off with a message from Harris:

Let's meet for dinner tonight around eight at the Yankee Clipper. Success calls for a celebration.

Chad carried the memory chip in his pocket all day. When he left work, it was still light outside. He stopped at the apartment, hoping Kristen would be home from work. Chad found her typing at her computer. "What are you doing?"

"Working on a feature for next week's edition. How was your day?"

"Excellent," Chad happily answered. "My human patients on the ward are doing well, and thankfully, so are Harris's tiny sick mice. It looks like they are going to make a full recovery. I'm meeting Gordon for dinner tonight around eight and give him the memory chip. Can you join us?"

"Where are you going?"

"The Yankee Clipper."

"Ooh—the best lobster in the city." Kristen glanced at her computer. "Sure, I'll come along."

They took a cab to the restaurant. Before entering, Chad instinctively looked over his shoulder for anything that seemed suspicious. He saw nothing unusual, so he opened the door for Kristen and they went inside. Harris, who was sitting at a booth in the far corner, stood and waved them over.

"It's good to see you again," Chad said to Harris, taking his mentor's hand and shaking it firmly. "Dr. Harris, do you remember Kristen?"

"Of course, from the Christmas party," Harris said. "That was well over a year ago, so…can I assume that this means there's something serious between you two?"

"I hope so," Kristen answered, glancing toward Chad and smiling.

Chad took the chip from his pocket and passed it to his friend. "Let me give you this now."

"So you saw...what was on it?"

"Yes," Chad answered, "I had to make sure they were giving me the real thing before I exchanged the mice for it."

"Then let me apologize for what you must have seen," Harris said, hanging his head low. "The only consolation I have is that it should help put an end to Celestica's plans." Harris paused, reached over, and patted Chad's shoulder. "I don't know how I can possibly thank you for all you've done. Kristen, I'm sure you realize you have a heck of a guy there."

"Agreed," she said, smiling.

"Anyway, I say we get a nice bottle of wine and order some dinner."

"Sounds great," Chad and Kristen responded in unison. Over their meal, the threesome reminisced and told stories. After the second bottle of wine, all their worries melted away. Harris excused himself to use the restroom, and after he returned to the table, they left. It was after eleven.

"Indulge me," Harris said, as they stood together outside the restaurant. "Let's walk up Beacon Hill. It'd be good for our digestion, and I'd like to pass by my old apartment. It isn't far."

"Sure," Chad answered. "A walk after the feast we just had sounds like a good idea." Kristen nodded. They started up the steep grade of Beacon Hill. As they neared the top, they saw a man was walking down toward them. He stopped directly in front of them, blocking their path. All three came to an abrupt halt.

"You again," Chad said, recognizing the man from the Common.

"Yeah, it's me." Flowers pulled a gun from his coat pocket. "I want all of you to head very calmly over to the car parked across the street."

Before anyone took a step, Kristen sprang forward. With a lightning-fast karate chop, she knocked the weapon out of the startled assailant's hand, then immediately spun around and kicked hard at his leg. A loud cracking sound indicated that she had found her mark. Flowers buckled and dropped to the pavement, clutching his broken lower extremity.

"Damn, you're good," Chad commented to Kristen, as he pushed the weapon that had fallen to the ground beyond the injured man's reach. While Flowers lay writhing in pain, Chad took out his cell phone and called for an ambulance.

Kristen, a little breathless after the encounter, said, "I guess now you wish you'd kept going to karate class."

"As long as I have you—" Chad never finished his statement. Instead, he suddenly asked, "Where's Gordon?" They looked around. Harris was gone.

"Let's get out of here," Chad suggested, and they ran down the hill.

By the time they reached Charles Street, the ambulance Chad had called turned the corner and rushed past them. Their evening, which had begun on such a high note, ended in utter disaster. Harris and the memory chip were gone. Chad realized that if it hadn't been for Kristen and her black belt they might have ended up as coroner's cases.

Chad hailed a cab and they headed home, drained. Once inside the apartment, he locked the door. A moment later his phone rang.

"Reynolds, listen carefully to what I tell you." It was Murdock on the other end. "I have Dr. Harris, and if you tell anyone about this, your doctor friend is history. You and your girlfriend just go about your usual activities, and forget about him." The line went dead.

Chad turned to Kristen. "They have Harris, and will kill him if we go to the police."

"But we have to do something!" Kristen pleaded. "I'm sure they're going to come after us again." She dropped onto the couch, thinking. After a few minutes she turned to Chad with a smile. "I have an idea."

18

Witig was hiking a glacial plain in the mountains above Grindelwald when his satellite phone went off. He removed his backpack and took the phone out. It was Anderson.

"Herr Witig. We have Dr. Harris."

"That's good news. You've made my day."

"Better yet, in a matter of hours, Harris will be on his way to Switzerland. Murdock has discussed the details with your security chief, Hans Spiegel. Harris's lab has already been packed up and shipped. He will continue his work at your headquarters after arrival." Anderson paused then went on. "I promised you a successful conclusion to the Juvena Project, and I intend to keep that promise."

"Jim, I'm not in the office," Witig laughed. "You caught me hiking in the mountains, but I'm pleased you called and even more pleased to hear that all those arrangements have been made."

"Herr Witig, I expect that by the time you return to Geneva, you will be able to say hello to Harris in person."

"Wonderful. You can also expect a nice bonus in your next paycheck."

"Thank you, Herr Witig. Goodbye for now."

Witig returned the satellite phone to his backpack and took out a set of ice picks. He picked up his pace, practically running across the glacier's icy terrain. He leapt over a crevasse, barely making it to the other side. Even with the ice picks, it was possible that next time a wider gap could swallow him. Witig knew he was playing a dangerous game, but it was that very element of danger he relished most.

**

A car drove up to the front gate at the Celestica American subsidiary. The guard stuck his head out the window of his station, and asked, "Can I help you?"

Chad was driving. "Nuclear Regulatory Agency, safety check," he said, flashing a badge borrowed from a friend, radiation physicist John Holmes at Boston General.

"Okay, Mr. Holmes. Go right ahead." The gate opened allowing him to drive in and park at the administrative building. His palms were sweating. To go along with playing the role, he had brought a Geiger counter and clipboard with a genuine radiation safety checklist. Chad walked up to the reception desk at Celestica headquarters wearing the official looking state agency badge and was asked to wait.

A few minutes later, a woman approached him. "Mr. Holmes," she said. "It's my pleasure to escort you around our facility."

They visited the labs where nuclear isotopes were used or stored, and Chad took measurements with his Geiger counter. "Everything seems to be in order so far," he told his guide, in an official sounding tone. "Just one issue—you need to label any rooms that hold nuclear material with signage indicating special caution to those who *might* be pregnant. It's a new regulation."

"That sounds quite reasonable," the woman said, jotting a note down on the pad of paper she held.

"I still need to see Building Four. My list indicates that there was a delivery of some radioactive material to that location in the last few weeks."

His guide hesitated. "Building Four is a secure area. Visitors are not allowed."

"Secure or not, the Nuclear Regulatory Agency says I need to check it out."

"I guess I can take you over. The last thing we want is a problem with the government."

They went to Building Four. Chad took radiation measurements and recorded his findings. In the basement, his guide unlocked a door and allowed Chad to enter a lab with empty shelves, cabinets, and countertops. It had the look of having been hastily cleared. Chad used his Geiger counter and scribbled some numbers down. Then he told his guide, "The space is empty, but I'm getting an elevated gamma signal in this room."

"Oh, the lab in here was just packed up and shipped to our main facility in Switzerland. Research on this project will be continued abroad."

With a serious look on his face, Chad said, "The high reading I'm getting indicates that there was a radiation spill here. I'll need to speak with the person who was conducting the research here."

"Sorry, but that won't be possible. He was transferred to our headquarters in Geneva."

"Are you certain?"

"Yes, I'm quite sure. I filled out the transfer forms myself."

Chad's mind was racing. "All right, the readings aren't *that* far off. What you need to do is post a sign on the door keeping people out of this room for another month. By then, the radiation decay should make it safe to reenter. I'll send you a certification letter after that."

"Well, Mr. Holmes, we appreciate your visit and thank you for the suggestions but I must say, I'm a bit surprised by your presence since our last inspection was only three months ago. I was told the next one wouldn't be for another six."

Chad felt his pulse quicken. "Yes, that's correct. But we do random site checks on all isotope users, regardless of when routine inspections occur."

"I see," the woman answered, appearing satisfied with his response.

Chad headed out the front gate of the Celestica complex. Harris had been taken to Switzerland and would probably be under tighter guard than ever. His stomach knotted on the drive back to Boston as he wondered what he could do to help his friend.

**

Anderson received a call. "You asked me to let you know when the DNA analysis on the mice was complete."

"Well then?"

"Those mice aren't even distant cousins of the ones we originally had."

"Are you sure? The serial numbers on their bellies match ours."

"Tattoos can be duplicated; DNA cannot. I'm absolutely certain. We ran the analyses twice."

"Thanks," Anderson said, slamming the phone down. Then he shouted, "Shit!" loud enough for his secretary to hear through the closed office door. Her intercom light blinked on. She picked up and Anderson barked, "Get Murdock for me on the phone, now!" When he called back, Anderson gave him the bad news, "Those sons of bitches. They switched the damn mice on us."

"Then I'll just have to visit Reynolds's lab myself and get the real ones."

19

"Did you find Harris?" Kristen anxiously asked when Chad returned from his visit to Celestica.

"He's not there. They've taken him to the company headquarters in Switzerland."

"Darn. What do we do now?"

"I'm not sure," Chad answered. "Harris and the memory chip are gone. Going to the police won't do much good."

"I agree. But, Chad, you don't seriously think those people are going to let us live happily ever after? You switched the mice on them. Unless we do something quickly to help Harris and protect ourselves, we won't be around very much longer, either."

"Maybe going on the offensive is the thing to do. What if I tried to get a confession from the man who pulled the gun on us? You busted his leg up pretty bad. I'll bet the ambulance that came took him to the nearest hospital, which means he's probably in an orthopedic ward at Boston General right now."

"But, we don't know his name."

"I think I can find out easy enough. Perhaps a hospital visit to our recuperating friend is in order."

Instead of going home after work the next day, Chad went to the medical records department. He typed his physician code into a computer station, gained access to the hospital's information system and checked the census on the orthopedics ward. There were forty-two inpatients listed with a variety of orthopedic problems, most of them hip or knee-replacement surgeries.

Chad scanned all the names for a man admitted from the ER on the previous evening. He found that the patient in room 836 had come into the ER that night with severe trauma to the lower extremity. The patient's operative procedure was listed as repair of fractured tibia, dislocated patella, and torn anterior collateral ligament—just the type of injury that could result from a hard karate-style kick to the shin.

The intake record indicated that the injury had been caused by a fall on slippery pavement while walking down Beacon Hill. "Bullshit! That's him. It has to be him." Chad checked through the patient's demographic profile: Earl Flowers; age, fifty-one; employer, Special Security Consultants. "Bingo!"

It was well past visiting hours, and the orthopedic ward was quiet when Chad exited the elevator and headed for Flowers's room. Wearing his white lab coat and Boston General ID, Chad looked every bit like an orthopedic surgeon making late rounds after a busy day in the operating room. Chad entered room 836. Sure enough, his left leg covered by a cast held in traction, was the man who had traded the memory chip for Harris's mice. It was the same man who said he hoped never to see Chad again, only to hold him at gunpoint later on. Chad would have given anything to have a picture of the shocked look on Earl Flowers's face when he saw who the doctor was standing at his bedside.

"How are you doing this evening, Mr. Flowers?" Chad queried as if he were the patient's real physician. The patient remained silent. His hand moved over toward the call button, but Chad beat him to it and pulled it out of his reach. "You don't need to call anyone Mr. Flowers. After all, your personal physician is already here at the bedside. Now please answer my question."

"I'll live."

"I need some information from you. If you give it to me, we can keep this visit a secret between us. Your boss at will never know about our meeting."

"What makes you think I'd tell you anything? Fuck you and that broad of yours who did this to me. If it wasn't for her, you wouldn't be standing there looking so smug."

"How would you like to go through another surgery on that injured leg of yours?"

"What do you mean?"

Chad lifted his arm and came down hard on the cast with a quick chop. Flowers screamed in pain. "I've worked in this hospital for years, so I know that no one can hear you through these insulated walls. Now, are you ready to talk to me?"

"Go to hell," Flowers answered.

Chad came down even harder with the second blow. Again Flowers cried out. "One more time, and I bet you'll be back in the operating room tomorrow."

"Okay, asshole. What is it you want to know?"

"Good. I'm glad you decided to be reasonable. I like patients who listen to what their doctors tell them." Chad stood menacingly above Flowers at the side of the bed. "Who gives you your instructions?"

"The head of Celestica's security detail, William Murdock."

"Where is Dr. Harris now?"

"He's been flown to the company headquarters in Geneva, Switzerland."

"What's his location there?"

"Heck if I know."

"What were you planning for me?"

"You're pretty smart. I'm sure you can figure that one out."

"What happened to the girl I saw in those photos, Claire?"

"That's not her real name, it's Susan Blaylock. Murdock gave her pure heroin so she would overdose. But you'll never find her," Flowers answered grinning. "I put her corpse in an industrial incinerator so there's nothing left but ash. Even a doctor should know that without a body there is no murder."

"Well, I think that covers what I needed to know."

"You won't tell Murdock about this? He'd kill me in a minute if he found out I talked to you."

"We'll see," Chad said, leaving the question unanswered as he walked out.

Down the corridor, Chad reached into the pocket of his lab coat, pulled out the micro-recorder that had captured his conversation with Flowers, and clicked it off. Now he had the evidence needed of murder even without the photo chip or body of the unfortunate murdered woman.

Flowers was eliminated as a danger for the time being and he wasn't going anywhere soon. His leg would keep him hospitalized or in rehab for a few more weeks. Once they got Harris safely away from Celestica, the recorded confession and Harris's testimony would be enough to put the company's criminals away. The big question remaining for Chad was how to get Harris safely back from Switzerland, and do it without losing his own life.

When he returned home, Chad played the recording for Kristen. After listening to Flowers's confession, she said, "Wow! You've really got the goods on them. Want to know something else? You'd make a damn good investigative reporter. And the more I think about it, this would make one heck of a story for the *Globe*."

"First, let me get Harris back from Switzerland in one piece. *Then* you can write about it."

"You mean let *us* get Harris back from Switzerland. You're not going there without me." Chad was going to argue, but Kristen cut him off. "And I think I have an idea that will work."

"Okay," Chad said, recognizing her tone. Fighting with her about not going would be fruitless.

"We can use my job as journalist to get into Celestica's Swiss headquarters. I'll pretend I'm doing a story for the *Globe*'s business section on pharmaceutical companies and want to include the parent company of the local American subsidiary. Getting into a newspaper article like that would be considered a plum by any business. It's invaluable free advertising."

"What will I do?" Chad asked.

"You'll be my photographer. It will play well, trust me," said Kristen. "We can get in, find Harris, and get him out."

"You seriously think we can pull this off?"

"I know we can."

"All right then," Chad said. He headed to his desk and rummaged through the drawers.

"What are you doing?" Kristen asked.

"I'm looking for...these." He turned to her, beaming, holding up their passports. "Start packing. We're going to Switzerland."

Later, Chad drove to the research facility to make sure Harris's mice were doing well. As he pulled up to the building, he noticed police cars with their lights flashing parked in front. Showing his hospital ID, Chad entered the building, and raced toward his office with a sense of dread. There was commotion down the hall. Police officers were milling around outside the door to his lab.

"Excuse me," Chad said to one of them. "I'm Dr. Reynolds, and that's my lab. What's going on?"

The policeman stopped writing on his pad and addressed him. "There's been an assault. A lab technician was messed up pretty bad. He's been taken to the emergency room."

"What was the tech's name?" Chad asked, fearful of the answer.

The officer looked down at his notes. "Percy Adams."

"Oh my God!" Chad exclaimed, shaken by the news. He struggled to compose himself. "Officer, can I look inside for a second?"

"Yeah, go ahead. Forensics has already been here and gone."

Chad looked for Harris's mice. The Plexiglas enclosure was gone! He went to the refrigerator and unlocked its door. The vials of Juvena were still there, but that was small comfort. Chad ran out of the lab, heading to the hospital to check on Percy.

He pushed through the door of the General's busy emergency room and ran up to the first nurse he saw. "Which exam room is Percy Adams in? He's a lab tech who was assaulted next door in the research building."

The nurse looked at Chad and shook her head. "Sorry, but he's not here anymore. The neurosurgeons took him to the OR a while ago."

"The OR—why?"

"He had a massive subdural from head trauma that needed immediate drainage. By now they probably finished his surgery and have him up in the ICU."

Chad rushed out of the ER and headed for the surgical ICU. When he entered Percy's room, Chad found him still unconscious, hooked up to a ventilator and with his head wrapped in gauze dressing. He approached the nurse at his bedside and cautiously asked, "How's Mr. Adams doing?"

"So far, so good," she answered. "The neurosurgical team came by just minutes ago to check on him, and said they think he has a good chance to make a full recovery."

"I sure hope so," Chad said, his voice cracking with emotion. "Please take special care of him. He's a dear friend." *Someone from Celestica must be behind this.* Chad recalled the name Flowers mentioned. *Murdock. William Murdock.*

20

Witig's private jet landed at Kinshasa airport. A limousine waiting on the tarmac picked him up for his meeting with Holfield. Witig traveled alone, without the usual business entourage of lawyers and accountants, because this meeting required strict privacy. As his limo entered the city limits, it was forced to negotiate the bustling traffic of cars, motorbikes, and pedestrians, so the driver could only proceed at a snail's pace. Witig grew progressively impatient. Finally, his frustration boiled over and he jumped out of the car, marching ahead on foot. Kinshasa's heat and humidity immediately engulfed him. He sighed with relief entering the air-conditioned interior of the capital's tallest building, where the Celestica regional office was located. Witig rode the elevator to the fifteenth floor where Paul Holfield awaited him.

As he came through the door, Holfield greeted him cheerfully. "Herr Witig, I'm so glad to see you. It was an excellent idea for us to go over the Juvena data one more time before you present it to the regulatory agency next week."

"Yes," Witig said curtly, still irritated from his scorching walk. "Let's get on with it."

Holfield pulled out a chair at the conference table for his boss. On the table, he unfolded the giant spreadsheet that tracked the two hundred fifty patients taking the experimental Juvena injections. "Herr Witig, you know better than anyone that a year of very hard work and a lot of money has gone into this study. One thing I can assure you—the investment has been well worth the cost."

Witig scanned the figures and graphs. "Can you give me a summary on the complications?"

"Of course," Holfield answered. "Three subjects developed a mild rash. Six had nausea. Four had local discomfort at the injection sites. No one had a complication severe enough to cause them to withdraw from the study."

Witig's face lit up, "I would call those results fantastic. The European Medicines Agency will be happy to hear that. It should make Juvena a shoo-in for approval."

"Well, as you know, there were those two cases—the two subjects who died when they stopped taking injections on their own. As you requested, I removed them from the data set."

"Excellent," Witig said, affirming the decision. "If they didn't follow the instructions as agreed to in the protocol, it should disqualify their inclusion."

"We compensated the families with a very generous amount of money."

"That was very nice of you, but those sad fools tried cheating us by stopping treatment after we paid for them to take a daily injection. In my opinion, they got what they deserved."

Holfield knew there wasn't a prayer for Juvena but he was going to put on a very different act in front of his company's head. Holfield had already given Jung detailed information about the two deaths related to the drug, and by now someone at the regulatory agency had seen it. That would be enough for a vote against approval. There would be a major corporate upheaval at Celestica once the news about Juvena's failure went public, and Holfield had no intention of being around when it happened. By then he would be collecting severance and enjoying himself in Monte Carlo. Later he planned to move into his new office in Bern as a key member of Gustav Jung's staff at Novara.

As their meeting was about to conclude, Holfield said, "Congratulations, Herr Witig. The approval of Juvena will mark a milestone Celestica's history. Unfortunately, with this great project completed, I must take this opportunity to inform you that I will be moving on."

"Oh, I'm so sorry to hear that," said Witig, feigning displeasure. "You've done such a brilliant job for our company. Is there a reason you can share?"

Holfield answered, "In all honesty, the hot dusty climate here has wreaked havoc with my asthma and allergies."

"Well, thank you for all your hard work. In fact, first thing tomorrow I will give my secretary, Inger, a call to arrange for a special bonus in addition to your severance. Just give her the routing and account number for where you want your money sent. She will wire it there before the end of the business day."

"You are too kind, Herr Witig," Holfield said, bowing graciously. "After your long trip here, I had been planning on a special evening of relaxation and entertainment for you."

"Regrettably, Paul, I must head back to Geneva tonight." With the Juvena Project data completed, Witig didn't need Holfield anymore, and he couldn't bear man's cocky attitude. If Holfield stayed on, he would just be another big salary on the payroll, so Witig had no intention of battling the man's decision to leave.

"Are you sure you have to go back tonight?" Holfield asked.

"Yes. Perhaps we'll celebrate some other time." Witig went on. "Let me wish you good luck in all your future endeavors. If you need a letter of recommendation for another job opportunity, please don't hesitate to let me know."

Witig walked out the door, leaving Holfield behind; grateful he would never have to visit godforsaken Kinshasa again.

21

I nger settled into the penthouse suite at the Grand Hotel in St. Moritz, their favorite spot for a quick getaway in the mountains. As soon as she unpacked the little luggage she had brought along, Inger dialed room service. "Can you bring up some champagne and caviar?"

"Your usual, madam?"

"That would be just fine."

She had more to do in preparation for her lover's arrival. Inger changed into one of his favorite outfits of hers: a translucent red bra with a skimpy matching thong and garter. She put on a pair of red velvet stiletto heels then touched up her makeup. Inger looked at herself in the full-length mirror and smiled contentedly. At thirty-five, she had the body of someone ten years younger, and that pleased her. Inger was ready for their rendezvous. A little fine dining, some drinking, then sex like there was no tomorrow.

She called Rolfe on his cell. "Darling, when will you be arriving?"

"I should be there within the hour."

"Good, I have a little treat for you."

"What might that be?" he asked inquisitively.

In a sexy voice, she answered, "I'll give you a hint. It's soft, warm, a little moist, and anxiously awaiting your arrival."

Glitzy St. Moritz was a far cry from the mountain hostels and sleeping huts they used when Inger accompanied Witig on his

Alpine treks. Inger had always been in superb physical condition. A skier since childhood, she had grown up in Oberstdorf, a mountain resort town in southern Germany not far from the Swiss border.

After taking the job as Witig's administrative secretary, Inger soon realized his great passion for climbing and saw a window of opportunity. On her vacation, she enrolled in the mountaineering school in Zermatt, at the foot of the Matterhorn. Not long after, when Witig called on the intercom and asked her to put a five-day trip to the Eiger on his calendar, she asked nonchalantly, "May I join you?"

At first Witig laughed, thinking it was a joke.

"I'm serious, Herr Witig. I can climb as well as anyone."

He was impressed by her confidence, but had no intention of being an accomplice to her falling down a mountainside. "Okay, Inger, but first you must pass my test." A few moments later, Witig came out of his office carrying a backpack, which he put on the desk in front of her. He went over the outer office door and locked it from the inside, telling Inger, "We must not be interrupted. The test will require your absolute concentration." He opened the backpack and took out climbing rope, carabineers, and a mountain harness.

"Tie a figure eight knot for me." Inger picked up the rope and finished the complex knot in seconds. Surprised at her success, Witig barked another request. "Now tie the other end with an alpine butterfly loop to the carabineer." Again, she completed the task in seconds.

Rolfe nodded his head in approval. "It seems you know the basics. Now, show me how you put on the climbing harness."

"Herr Witig," said Inger, looking at him steadily. "I can't very well do that with a dress on, can I?"

"How badly do you want to go climbing?"

Her answer came as she unzipped the side of her dress and let it drop to the floor. Witig sucked in his breath at the sight of her beautiful long legs, skimpy bikini underwear, and exposed breasts. Inger's body was simply gorgeous.

Shamelessly half naked, she picked up the harness, put each leg in the proper loop, positioned the waistband at a proper height, and then cinched it tight. Finished, Inger looked up at Witig. "Do I pass?"

"Yes, I give you an A!"

Inger stepped forward, put her arms around his neck, and kissed him deeply on the mouth. He responded. Lifting her up from the waist by the harness, continuing the kiss, he carried her to the sofa in the reception area. In moments, without removing the harness, Witig was inside her.

**

For their ascent of the Eiger, Witig chose the easiest way up. The more challenging route was on the nearly vertical north face, and not meant for an inexperienced climber like Inger. Nearing the summit, they stopped to rest on a prominent ledge that left them a comfortable margin of safety. Both were exhilarated by the intoxicating effect of the thin atmosphere, bright alpine sunshine, and view of quaint Zermatt nestled far below. Soon they had removed enough clothing to make love against a giant slab of dark granite that radiated the sun's warmth to their bodies.

In the midst of their passion, they heard loud clattering and glanced over in the direction of the sound. A magnificent white ibex appeared from behind a crag. It halted briefly to stare at them, seeming to question what right humans had to invade its mountain domain. Then, with a single energetic leap, the ibex flew to another ledge and was gone. Witig was still inside her. Looking at each other they laughed, continuing with their lovemaking as if never interrupted.

**

Chloe, Witig's ex-wife, was French and a delicate beauty. The aristocratic match between them had been made to cement the relationship of her family, which controlled the giant French drug concern Sanofte, with his, which ran Celestica. With her degree in fashion design from the Sorbonne and plenty of money at her disposal, Chloe was a devotee of couture. When Witig went off on a trek, she headed for Paris, Milan, or London on a shopping spree; Chloe abhorred anything to do with mountains. It wasn't long before they divorced. Fortunately, they had done so before children came along to complicate the rupture.

After Chloe, he vowed never to marry again. Inger told Witig that it didn't matter to her whether they were married or not, as she had all she wanted in their relationship. Inger accompanied him to all major corporate events as if she were his wife. Their relationship was an entirely open affair.

Witig opened the door of their suite at the Grand Hotel carrying in his briefcase. He wore an elegant suit and tie, having come to St. Moritz directly from a meeting with bankers in Zurich. Inger was on him in a second. She pulled off his jacket then pushed him down onto the bed, her hands sliding up his chest to undo his tie. Next she straddled him and began unbuttoning his shirt.

"Hold on a second," Witig said. "You told me on the phone you have a treat for me, so I brought one for you." He slid out from under her and got up to open his briefcase. Reaching inside, Witig removed an envelope then spilled its contents onto the bed in front of Inger. A few small yellow pills rolled onto the silken sheets.

"What are those?"

"It's from our research department. To be specific, it's $C_{13}H_{18}NO_2$. We don't have a marketing name yet."

Inger laughed, "That doesn't mean a damn thing to me, Rolfe."

"Ah, that may be true now, but soon it could mean a lot. These pills are part of Celestica's next venture after Juvena. It's a completely legal version of MDMA, the drug commonly known as Ecstasy. The addition of a single strategically placed methyl group makes all the difference. Ecstasy's bad side effects go away, while the pleasure it gives is enhanced. Best of all, it's not habit forming. I thought you might enjoy trying some out."

"Darling, you think of everything, don't you?"

Inger went over to the bottle of chilled Dom Pérignon and poured the bubbly golden liquid into two crystal flutes. She put some caviar on toast wedges and, sitting on his lap, fed one to Witig. After the snack, each took one of the little yellow pills, swallowing it with more champagne. While Witig had the where-withal, he put the "Do Not Disturb" sign outside the door of their room. Minutes later, the drug started taking effect. The two had their clothes off and were playfully chasing each other around the suite. When Witig caught Inger, he picked her up and put her over his shoulder. Marching over to the bed, he threw her onto the soft down comforter, then dove next to her. The chemical agent they had taken gave their bodies heightened sensation, which magnified their sexual energy. Witig buried his head between Inger's breasts, then tore off her skimpy red thong to enter her. A few minutes later, she was on top, relishing the position above, until he flipped her over and took her from behind. Inger moaned with pleasure, burying her face into the soft down comforter as she and her lover reached climax simultaneously.

Large floor-to-ceiling windows at the foot of their bed yielded an unparalleled view of the Alps lit up under a full moon. However, after ravenous sex, the lovers slept soundly, oblivious to the amazing beauty of the mountain peaks in front of them.

22

Lance Weber, a staff photographer at the *Globe*, picked up the phone in his office. It was Kristen calling. "Lance, I need to ask you for a favor," she said. "And it's a big one."

"Sure, Kristen, what's up?"

"Chad and I are going abroad for a few days for a story, and I wondered if we could borrow some of your camera equipment? I have a cheap 35 mm digital, but nothing professional-looking. Chad has to look like a real photographer."

"I see," Lance said. "He has to *look* like a real photographer? Kristen, you know I like you—but I *don't* like lending out my best cameras or lenses. I've been burned too many times in the past. What are you trying to do, turn your boyfriend into a professional photographer and put me out of a job?"

"Lance, I guarantee you have nothing to worry about as far as your job goes. And I promise we'll take good care of any gear we borrow."

"I might be able to loan you some things, but only if you level with me about what's going on. Is this something I should be covering?"

"No, it's not really about the photos. It's about the story, and the prospect of a photo shoot will help me get the access I need," said Kristen. "You know, maybe it *is* best if someone I trust knows where we're going and why, so I'll tell you. But for now, this stays between us. We're leaving tomorrow for Switzerland to do an investigative piece on a crooked pharmaceutical company. Chad is posing as my photographer."

"Well, when it comes to the photos, you'll probably end up getting exactly what you paid for. The cameras are incredible, but the photos will only be as good as the person who takes them—and that takes training and experience. Are you sure you don't want me to come along?"

"No, we're footing the bill on this, not the *Globe*. So, although I'm sure your right, Chad will have to do. What to do say, Lance, will you help? Please?"

"Okay, I suppose I could make an exception for you. I'll lend him my spare bag, a flash, a lens or two and *maybe* a camera. Have Chad stop by tomorrow morning. I'll get some things prepared. I can show him a few essentials, like how to put the camera and lenses together, check the lighting to get the best exposure, use the flash. Assuming he's a pretty bright guy, learning the basics shouldn't take that long."

"Lance, you're the best," Kristen said. "Oh, just one more thing, Chad needs a press ID badge."

"Now *that's* a tall order on short notice. But I guess I can put something together that should work for your purposes. E-mail me his photo right away, and I'll give him one of my older ones with his picture doctored onto it."

"Can you have it by tomorrow?"

"I'll do my best. By the time he stops by the office, I should have his ID ready for him."

"The picture will be on its way as soon as we get off the phone."

"Okay. If I don't talk to you again before you leave, have a safe and successful trip."

"Lance, thanks a million. You're a real sweetheart."

"Just bring my stuff back in working order and I'll be happy."

Kristen hung up the phone. She didn't expect Chad to win a Pulitzer with the pictures he took on their trip. It would be enough if he acted like he knew what he was doing with a professional camera and lens in his hands.

In the morning, Chad and Kristen left home earlier than usual. They went out the back door, in case anyone was watching the front. Each carried only a backpack, so nothing looked out of the ordinary. Chad headed for the hospital to leave word with his team he had to be out of town for a few days, then took a cab for the *Boston Globe* to meet up with Lance.

"You'll need this if you really want to look like a pro," Lance said, extending his hand to display all the equipment he had arranged on a table.

"Look, I've got this camera of Kristen's, but the only setting I know how use is automatic," said Chad, looking at the equipment with dismay. "I don't even know what half that stuff is for." He handed the camera to Lance.

"Awesome—you have the same lens mount. That simplifies things. So I'll give you a second camera, these two lenses, a retractable reflection umbrella, a light meter, and these memory chips."

Chad wondered how he could lug all the gear around, let alone learn how use it.

Lance noticed the overwhelmed look on Chad's face and reassured him, "Don't worry, sixty minutes from now, I'll have you using this stuff like a pro." Chad shook his head in disbelief then responded, "But, it looks more complicated than the instrument table in an operating room at the General."

"Well, imagine this is my operating room. Let me show you how to do photographic surgery." Both men laughed. Lance taught Chad how to swap lenses, use the light meter, and set up the umbrella. He explained the basic settings on the cameras, described the best uses for the different lenses, and handed him a small cheat sheet that covered the basics for Chad to read on the plane. "Okay, now for your practical examination. I know you medical jocks have a saying, 'See one, do one, teach one.' So now it's time for step two. Show me how you put it all together. Take my picture and make me look good."

Chad swapped out the telephoto for the normal lens. He set up a chair at a right angle to the natural light streaming in through the window, and motioned Lance into it. He set up the umbrella reflector to fill in the shadows and then placed his camera on the telescoping tripod. Using the timer, he shot a bracket of frames. Afterward he showed the results to Lance in the display screen. "Not bad," Lance said with a smile. "Now, for one last thing, we've got to get you looking like a real photographer." Lance handed him a vest with multiple pockets and loops. After Chad put it on, Lance picked up two cameras and hung them so they crisscrossed his chest. He clipped the strap of the light meter to the vest and slipped the memory chips into one of the Velcro pockets. Lance packed the rest of the delicate gear into a worn travel case and slung the strap over Chad's left shoulder.

"Well, what do you think?" Lance's student inquired, the equipment hanging from him like ornaments on a Christmas tree.

"Hmmm…" Lance responded, contemplating his work. "I have to admit, you look like a real paparazzo. You've earned your diploma." Going to his desk Lance took out the press ID badge he had made for Chad. He hung the lanyard over his neck. "Now you are the genuine item!" Lance proclaimed, pleased with his creation.

**

While Chad collected his gear from Lance, Kristen was already on her way to Logan airport. She had her laptop, satellite phone, note pads, and recorder in her backpack—everything she needed to play the reporter she actually was. She also brought along a fake press ID, one she used when doing anonymous snooping. On this trip she would be Rebecca Thomas, freelance reporter for the *Boston Globe*.

The cab dropped her off at the entrance to the international terminal. If all went according to plan, Chad would meet her there shortly, and in two hours they would be on a flight to Switzerland.

23

Chad and Kristen boarded their jet. They were flying to Frankfurt then taking a short connector to Geneva. As the jet taxied down the runway and took off, Chad looked out the window at the city below. He watched as the footprint of Boston General's giant campus shrink in the distance.

A flight attendant made sure they were comfortable then offered drinks. Sipping his Chardonnay, Chad turned to Kristen. "Say, do you happen to have any idea how we are going to find Harris once we get into Celestica's headquarters?"

"Don't worry," Kristen told him in a confident tone. "I think I've got that worked out."

"Could you please share those thoughts with me?"

"We've got a long flight ahead of us. There's plenty of time to go over everything. We've got to hit the ground running, so how about we rest first and talk later?"

Kristen put her head on Chad's shoulder and was out in a flash. Chad tried to sleep, but his mind wouldn't rest. He knew the people who held Harris were ruthless. Surely they wouldn't hesitate to kill again if someone tried to interfere with their plans, which was exactly what they intended to do. Chad was not reassured knowing that with the equipment he carried, the only things he could shoot were photos.

**

It was 2:30 a.m. when Murdock and one of his men approached the building on Marlboro. After picking the exterior lock, they walked up the stairs, planning to enter Reynolds's apartment then kill him and his girlfriend, asleep in bed. Before leaving, the two would trash the apartment and take any valuables to make it look like a robbery.

In the hallway, they donned night-vision goggles and screwed silencers onto their guns. Murdock picked the lock on the apartment door and the pair moved silently toward the bedroom, then fired repeatedly into the mounds on the bed. Murdock stepped forward and peeled back the covers to check his victims.

He found only pillows.

"Shit!" The two men looked at each other, mystified, still wearing their night vision goggles. *Where the fuck are they?*

24

Chad was awakened by the flight attendant. "Would you like your meal now? We will be landing in another hour."

"Sure, I'll have something to eat."

"No, thanks, not right now," Kristen answered. She had been up reading about Geneva from a guidebook on the plane. Chad gave her a quizzical look. "No reason we can't mix a little plea-sure with our business," she said. "It's not like we get to go to Europe all the time."

As Chad ate, Kristen read him some of the highlights from the travel guide. "Geneva, Switzerland, has strong French and German influences, since it borders both countries. You may even hear Italian spoken there. In contrast to the stereotype view of the Swiss as stodgy, Geneva inhabitants are often inclined to partake in the many urban activities this cosmopolitan city has to offer." She turned to Chad. "Do you think we'll have any fun during our visit?"

He half smiled at her. "Fun? I just hope we leave Geneva alive."

**

Murdock phoned Anderson first thing in the morning. He knew the conversation was not going to be a pleasant one.

"Did you take care of things?" Anderson asked.

"Not exactly."

"What do you mean?"

"They were gone. No one was at the apartment when we made our visit, and I have no idea where they are."

"Well, dammit. Find them and kill them. Understand?"

"It will be my pleasure." Murdock answered, steaming under the collar at Anderson's rudeness.

**

As the sun rose, their jet flew over the southern tip of Lac Léman, otherwise known as Lake Geneva, on its approach for landing. They had no luggage, only backpacks, so very soon after deplaning and passing through customs, they used the bank of phones to make reservations at a nondescript hotel, then got into a cab and rode to city center.

Once inside their room, Kristen set her backpack down and flopped onto the comfortable bed, kicking off her shoes. She sighed with pleasure at being engulfed by the thick down comforter. Chad followed her example, and soon they were pulling off each others' clothes. As rays of early morning sunlight filtered into the room, they made love.

**

Witig had a breakfast meeting with Oscar Becker, the Geneva head of research and development. Becker was slicing cheese while discussing progress on Juvena. "We finally have all the field safety data Holfield sent us for the upcoming European Medicines Agency presentation." Becker put a piece of cheese and cracker in his mouth, then pulled a sheet of paper from his portfolio and handed it to Witig.

Witig glanced over the numbers not giving any indication he had already seen them in Kinshasa with Holfield. "Excellent, Becker, excellent." Then he noted, "I see you have included the signed agreement with Harris giving Celestica exclusive rights to Juvena in the filing?"

"Yes, just as you requested."

"Good, Becker, that's very good."

**

Witig spoke with Anderson on the phone, "Can you believe Harris has is still trying to convince me to restrict use of Juvena to children with progeria?"

"He's been one unrealistic, stubborn, son of a bitch. If he'd only taken our first offer, things would have been so much easier."

"Yes, and in spite of all the trouble he caused we still have no choice but to pay Harris the three million in order to avoid suspicion." Witig chortled. "Of course, the fool will never see one penny of it. The money will end up going to his estate."

25

Witig wanted to smooth things out with Gustav Jung. He still planned to make a bid for ownership of Novara as soon as profits from Juvena started rolling in, but he wanted Jung to have good feelings toward him. The last thing Witig needed was a hostile CEO opposing his planned acquisition. That could mean years of expensive litigation, so he set up a meeting to make nice with his rival.

When his guest entered the boardroom, Witig smiled politely and greeted him. "Gustav, it's so good of you to accept my invitation."

"Glad to be here. I wouldn't miss an opportunity for lunch with my *dear friend* Rolfe."

"Come, let's have a drink." Witig graciously pulled out a chair for his guest. The boardroom's enormous table was laid out with a magnificent buffet. Witig asked, "May I pour you some wine? I had a bottle of Château Lafite Rothschild '96 brought in from my personal cellar for this special occasion. I think you'll like it."

"Thank you. That would be very nice. Lafitte '96—things must be looking up here at Celestica."

Witig ignored the statement. After pouring wine, he raised his glass for a toast. "To a better relationship between us...and our two great companies." Before he took his first sip, Witig added, "And, of course, to the continued good health of my esteemed guest."

Jung didn't dislike his rival; he just didn't care much for people who, like Witig, had never had to work hard for their positions in life, yet considered themselves peers with those who had. Jung had fought every step of the way to make it to the top. His father had been a longshoreman. As a child, Jung played among the cargo containers in the harbor at Hamburg. The workers took a liking to him, and soon discovered his special talent: Gustav could memorize a ship's manifest in a minute. When the foreman couldn't locate an item, he called for him over the loudspeaker. The boy would then scamper through the maze of freight containers and find the sought-after cargo, earning a few deutschemarks for his efforts. As a teenager, he toiled during summer vacations alongside his father doing manual labor on the dock. Gustav Jung was a man who had learned the true value of money through his own hard work and sweat.

It wasn't a secret to Jung that Witig had ambitions to take over his company, but he decided to play along before turning the tables. Jung looked out the picture window. "What a magnificent view. My office has an excellent view as well…of the smokestack at our plant, not Lac Léman." Both men laughed.

"Well, you must come and visit more often."

"That would be nice, but with my workload…I'm always running behind. There's not enough time for me to eat lunch most days."

"Gustav! All work, and no play—that's not a good formula. Let me offer you my chalet in Grindelwald for a weekend. It's a perfect place to get away and unwind."

"Grindelwald? Isn't that where your grandfather started the business?"

"Yes, and it was my home as a child," said Witig. "That is where I learned to love the mountains."

"Well, thank you for your offer, but I'm not one for the higher elevations," said Jung. "I get altitude sickness quite easily. I'm originally from Hamburg and grew up by the sea. Let me turn your invitation around. Why don't you come spend some time on my yacht? It berths in Monte Carlo, and can sleep ten comfortably. I will have it put at your service any time you wish."

"Unfortunately, I get motion sickness even on calm waters. The sea and I are not cut out for each other. Perhaps we don't share the same passions outside of our work, but at least we have one very important thing in common."

"What might that be?" Jung asked, perplexed.

"Our love of healthy corporate profits."

They laughed and continued with lunch while each man was thinking the very same thing. *You won't be laughing, once I own your company.*

26

Kristen went over the plan in the hotel room with Chad one last time. He listened intently then commented. "It sounds good. Let's just hope it works."

"It will work," she said. "It has to, right?"

Kristen picked up the telephone and called Celestica Pharmaceutical. An operator answered.

"May I speak with Rolfe Witig?" she asked.

"Please hold while I connect you."

Inger Kroll picked up. "Hello, Herr Witig's office. May I help you?"

"My name is Rebecca Thomas. I'm a reporter from the *Boston Globe* in the United States, and I'm writing an article about the pharmaceutical industry."

"I see. And what can I do for you, Ms. Thomas?"

Kristen answered, "I'm in Geneva at the moment, and before heading on to Basel, I was hoping to include Celestica in my piece—maybe feature the company because of your subsidiary near Boston. I would love to visit your facility. Perhaps I could even meet Herr Witig for a brief interview and photo shoot."

"Hold on while I check his schedule." A minute later Inger came back on the line. "Herr Witig has a small window of free time this afternoon. Can you be here at three o'clock?

"That would be wonderful."

"Do you need directions to our facility?"

"No, we have a map, thank you. I will be bringing a photographer, Lance Weber, if that is all right." Kristen continued. "Should we ask for you when we arrive?"

"Yes, that's fine. Just ask for, Inger Kroll. I am Herr Witig's administrative assistant."

"Terrific," Kristen said. After hanging up, she turned to Chad with a look of satisfaction on her face. "Done, we have an appointment at Celestica Pharmaceutical—this afternoon at three."

"Kristen, you never cease to amaze me."

"Thanks. I hope you still feel that same way ten years from now." She walked over and gave him a kiss. "We have some time to kill until our meeting." Kristen suggested, "Why don't we take a walk and see some of the city sights? You can practice with the camera gear."

"Good idea."

They walked along the Promenade du Lac and into the Jardin Anglais, where Chad took photos of Kristen near the flower clock, feeding the swans from the bank of Lac Léman, and against the backdrop of the majestic Jet d'Eau, Geneva's signature fountain, as it shot water nearly five hundred feet into the sky. They walked several blocks to have lunch at Le Café Papon, with its vaulted seventeenth-century ceiling. Afterward the couple headed back for the hotel to freshen up, then got into their rented Peugeot and drove off for the appointment with Witig.

Chad took the autobahn, heading north, out of the city. In forty-five minutes, they reached their destination. A security guard greeted them at the Celestica front gate. "Ah, yes, we were expecting you," he said with a friendly smile. "Ms. Kroll notified you would be coming." The guard gave each of them identity cards. "Let me show you how to get to the main administrative building. It can be a little tricky." He traced his finger along a route on the facility map he handed to Chad. "It's about two kilometers up this road."

Chad commented, "This place looks as big as the city of Geneva."

"Not quite," the guard answered.

When it came into view, the structure was impressive. From the outside it looked more like a museum of modern art than an administrative office building for a pharmaceutical company. Kristen spoke to a receptionist at the entry, making a request for Inger Kroll, from Herr Witig's office. Moments later a tall blonde emerged from an elevator behind the receptionist's desk.

"Hello, and welcome to you both," she said enthusiastically, speaking perfect English with a noticeable German accent. "I'm Inger Kroll. We talked on the phone." She extended her arm in greeting, and gave a firm handshake, first to Kristen, then Chad.

"Thank you so much for arranging our visit on such short notice," Kristen said.

"My pleasure," Inger answered. "Let's begin in my office."

Inger led the way to an elevator. Kristen carried a slim leather portfolio and a micro-recorder. Chad followed, with two cameras and his press ID hung around his neck and the carry bag containing the other equipment slung over one shoulder. The three exited on the top floor. On the way down the hall to her office, Inger asked, "Have you been enjoying your trip to Switzerland?"

"Yes, so far everything has been wonderful." Kristen said, "Unfortunately, there hasn't been much of a chance to sight-see yet. We've only been in your beautiful country for a few days and have yet to make stops in Basal and Zurich after this."

Inger told them, "Well, there are so many wonderful things to see and do in Switzerland. The only requirement is time, and perhaps money."

Entering the office, she offered them a chair and sat down behind her desk. Inger made a quick phone call then turned to her guests, "Well, I hope you're not too disappointed, but for the time being you will have to settle for speaking with me. Herr Witig's meeting is still in progress. In the meantime, what can I tell you about Celestica Pharmaceutical?"

Kristen quickly scanned through notes she had prepared for her interview, "I know the basics, but I'm hoping for a richer back-story—something more than just dates and milestones, you know?" she said. "For instance, I know the company has been in business since 1926, but how did it get started?"

"Anchel Witig, the grandfather of our current CEO, Rolfe, trained as a chemist in Vienna. After that, he returned home to Grindelwald and established a small apothecary. From that small village store that housed our founder's business, as well as his family, grew Celestica, this massive facility that we now occupy. That original apothecary is now a museum. New employees are required to visit so they can gain an appreciation of the great sense of tradition that permeates our company. Perhaps you can stop by there as well." She turned to Chad, smiling as he clicked her photo. "Grindelwald is *very* photogenic."

"Does Celestica involve itself in community activities?" Kristen inquired.

"The Witig family has been extremely philanthropic through the years. They support scores of local charities and are committed to reinvesting a sizable portion of profits to benefit those who work hard in helping Celestica achieve its success."

"Your employee turnover rate is rather low for the industry. What can you tell me about that?"

"It was started as a family business, and of course we still feel like family. The people who work for Celestica have never found the need to form a union. Full health care and subsidized housing is available for the asking. The company has even built schools and supported hiring outstanding teachers so that the children of our workers can enjoy the best possible education."

Kristen took notes. She looked up as Inger finished speaking. "Celestica's commitment to the local community seems quite extraordinary. Can we assume the company would have the same approach with its subsidiary in the United States?"

"Yes, to the extent possible," Inger answered, smiling. "Your country is somewhat less progressive in the areas of health and education, but we do what we can, of course. Although our company is publicly traded, the Witig family still controls most of its

stock. In the past the Witig family has resisted generous offers to
sell, out of concern that new owners might not share the family's
commitment to employees."

Kristen said, "That sounds highly commendable. Do you
think it will be much longer before I can meet Herr Witig?"

Inger looked at her watch. "I expect him to be free shortly.
His meeting should be finished very soon. Perhaps I can tell you
about our exciting research and development program, to pre-
pare you for the tour?"

"Sure," Kristen answered.

"Celestica has two stalwart drugs used around the world for
treatment of diabetes and hypertension. Regrettably, we are
perhaps better known for an innovative drug we developed for
pain control. Quellinol was extremely effective, but we withdrew
it from the market when a very small number of patients developed liver complications. Currently, our scientists are attempting to modify its chemical structure to eradicate the side effect
and bring the drug back in the future."

"I understand there are serious concerns about the company's financial health in view of its costly failure with Quellinol?"

Inger squirmed in her seat. "Well, we certainly have experienced some challenges. However, we have great faith in the
abilities of our senior management, and especially in Herr Witig,
to guide us through what has been a rather difficult period. Our
American subsidiary, for example, represents a major investment
to ensure a bright future through acquisition of new drugs for
our pipeline. With all the talent and research going on in the
vicinity of Boston, we should soon have a host of promising new

Kristen made her face a mask of innocence. "I recently heard
a rumor that the newest drug Celestica is planning to release
slows aging. Can you confirm that for me?"

new class of antibiotic agents to combat drug-resistant infections.

Perhaps that is what you heard about? As for any drug specific to aging, I'm unfamiliar with such plans…but wouldn't that be a wonderful idea!" Inger flashed a brilliant smile.

"A new class of drug to fight resistant infections—that sounds very promising," Kristen said, jotting more notes on her pad.

Inger knew that there were very few people privy to knowledge of Juvena. She was unsettled. "Can I ask where you heard the rumor about a drug that slows aging?"

"I wish I could tell you, but as a reporter, I am obligated to protect the confidentiality of my sources."

"Of course, I understand." Inger continued. "Please excuse me while I check on Herr Witig's status." She placed a call to his office but he didn't answer. Inger had to let Rolfe know that the reporter mentioned Juvena before his interview.

"It looks as though Herr Witig's meeting is lasting longer than anticipated. Why don't I take you on a tour of our facility in the meantime?"

"That sounds great," Kristen answered, nodding her head in approval.

"Could I ask you to meet me back at the reception area where you came in? I will join you there in ten minutes, and we can begin our tour." The visitors walked to the elevator and returned to the first floor where they sat and waited. Chad took some photos to pass the time.

Witig was in the midst of trying to convince a group of investment bankers that Celestica's future prospects were bright. His hard work at personal diplomacy had strung along several major banks that continued to stand behind his company in spite of its reversal with Quellinol. Now Witig sat in the conference room surrounded by posters of graphs he used to make key points in his presentation. The lines on each graph pointed in the same direction, upward. Witig desperately needed to maintain Celestica's current credit lines, at least for a little longer. Once Juvena was on the market, everything would be very different. Witig looked forward to the day he would never again have to grovel at the feet of arrogant bankers.

Inger's call to his private cell phone interrupted the presentation. Witig was irritated, but tried not to show it. He addressed his guests, smiling. "Excuse me, gentlemen. I will only be a moment." He left the meeting room and walked into his adjacent office.

She was waiting there as he came through the door. "For God's sake, Inger," he hollered. "You know better than to interrupt me during an important meeting."

"Rolfe, there is something you must know right away. An American reporter is here to interview you. She wants to do a story on us and our branch outside Boston."

"Well, that sounds very nice—we could use some free publicity—but that's hardly of significance at the moment."

"Yes, I agree. But, Rolfe, she asked about Juvena."

Witig saw the worried look on Inger's face. "By name?"

"No, just as a drug that slows aging.'"

"So, there must be a leak somewhere," he said matter-of-factly. "Perhaps someone at the advertising agency has been talking too much. Did you ask her how she came about that information?"

"Of course, but she claimed confidentiality of her sources."

Witig scowled at first then brightened. "Well, perhaps this is a good time to use the leak for our own purposes."

"What do you mean?"

"Next week I am presenting the clinical trial data for Juvena's approval. At that point, it will become public knowledge. Why not feed the reporter some information *now* that will get our marketing campaign off to a head start? A positive piece in the media early on could only help, right? What's more, our bankers will be pleased to see an article like that as well. Anything that makes them happy makes me happy."

"In that case, should I set her up for a longer meeting with you tomorrow?"

"That sounds like a very good idea."

"I can have them stop by tomorrow at ten. Your calendar is clear from then until the late afternoon."

"Excellent. For now, just take them on the usual tour and be a gracious hostess."

"Okay, my dear," Inger said. Approaching him, she rubbed her body affectionately against his and kissed him on the lips. As Witig turned to leave, Inger added, "And don't forget about our dinner plans."

"Of course not," he answered, as the door closed behind him.

27

Inger exited the elevator and approached Kristen. She told the reporter and her colleague, "I have both good and bad news. The good news is that Her Witig is anxious to see you. However, his important meeting is still in progress and looks like it will be for some time. With that being the case, he requested I free up his schedule for several hours tomorrow.

Could you be back, let's say, at ten in the morning? Then you can spend as long as you like together."

"That would be wonderful," Kristen answered. "It should give me more than enough time to get all the information I need."

"Well, with that understood, let's get on with a tour of our facility."

Inger drove Kristen and Chad in a motorized cart to see Celestica's main plant. When they arrived, they all donned white jumpsuits to walk through the location where most of the company's drugs were formulated. Large stainless steel vats filled with the raw materials from which drugs were formulated spun like tops in one of the large rooms they visited. Inger told her guests, "Five hundred thousand tablets and capsules are produced in this plant each day. Ultimately, the medications will be shipped to pharmacies in almost every country around the world."

"That's mind-boggling," Kristen said, impressed by the numbers. "Lance, can you get a photo of Ms. Kroll here in front of the company sign?"

"Of course." Inger primped, then allowed the photographer to position her.

"Excellent lighting. These will be great shots!" Chad proclaimed, snapping several pictures. "I'll send you a copy if you like."

"Thank you," Inger said. "That would be most kind."

"You can model for me any time," Chad said with a wink, causing Inger to blush.

After leaving the main plant, the three continued the journey around the property in the motorized cart. They passed a turnoff that led to a building with a substantial footprint on the facilities map. "What's in that huge building?" Kristen inquired, pointing in the direction of the turnoff.

"Oh, that's a research unit. That requires special clearance." Inger went on. "We work on antibiotics over there. They use live, infectious organisms, so visiting poses a risk of exposure. Nonemployees are strictly forbidden to go there without weeks of advance paperwork."

Kristen glanced at Chad. Clearly they were both thinking the same thing. *If Harris was anywhere on the grounds, it was there, in the building they wouldn't be allowed to see.*

When the mobile tour finished, Inger drove them to their rental car and dropped them off. "Hope you found your visit informative. I look forward to seeing you again tomorrow at ten."

"You've been most kind to spend so much time with us," said Kristen. "The Celestica facility is, to say the least, very impressive."

Inger seemed pleased by the compliment. "By the way, as long as you two are out this way, I suggest you have dinner at an enchanting place nearby that Herr Witig and I love. It's on your way back to the city. I insist you visit there as our guests."

"Why, thank you. That sounds lovely." Kristen glanced over at Chad and smiled.

She wrote out the directions and handed them to Kristen. "When you get to Le Château, ask for Kurt. He will take good care of you." Then Inger bid her guests goodbye. "Until tomorrow," she said, heading away in the cart.

On their way back to Geneva, Kristen and Chad stopped at Le Château. It was a charming old castle, restored and converted to a restaurant and hotel. Kurt, the manager, greeted them as they entered. "Monsieur Weber, Mademoiselle Thomas, I have been expecting you. Madame Kroll called on behalf of Herr Witig and asked that I look after you. Please, if you would follow me."

Kurt led them to a table with a breathtaking view of Lake Léman and the Alps. Over dinner, they quietly discussed their impression of the day's events. "Celestica is quite a company, when you think about it," Kristen noted. "The Witig family has run it successfully for over eighty years. They seem to have such a positive attitude toward their workers and the community." She lowered her voice until it was barely audible. "It's a shame they've turned to blackmail and murder. So, what are your thoughts about Harris?"

"Well, I think we can agree that he is most likely being held in that building we weren't allowed to visit, right?"

Kristen nodded. "We'll have to figure some way to get in there. But we can talk about that later, in the room," she said, as the waiter brought their food. "For now, let's enjoy the dinner. After all, Celestica is paying for it."

By the time they returned to their hotel, it was late. However, Kristen had something special in mind, and it wasn't plotting Harris's escape. She went into the bathroom. A minute later the door swung slowly open revealing Kristen standing in a sexy lavender chemise.

Chad's eyes widened. "Wow!"

"You told me to pack light. Is this light enough?"

Chad was standing next to the bed. Kristen approached, putting her arms around his neck. They fell onto the bed together. Kristen kissed him as he reached up under her chemise then began to fondle her breasts. She softly whispered into her lover's ear, "After a hard day of investigative reporting, this is exactly the way it should end."

As they made love, concerns about the daunting task ahead faded away.

28

They were up early. Chad put on the vest and gathered up his photography paraphernalia while Kristen prepared her recorder and portfolio. When they arrived at Celestica, the guard let them proceed through the gate without delay. Chad already knew the route, so he drove directly toward the administrative building. Inger was waiting outside for them at the entry. "Good morning to both of you. Did Kurt take good care of you last evening?"

Kristen answered, "Oh, yes. We had a terrific dinner at Le Château. The view from our table was nothing short of magnificent."

"I'm glad to hear you enjoyed yourselves," Inger said. "Now, we go to meet Herr Witig." She led them to the elevator. Once more, they rode it to the top floor, but this time they passed through Inger's office to Witig's. Inger extended her hand toward a tray of beverages and snacks. "Please, help yourselves. Herr Witig will be with us shortly."

Minutes later, Celestica's CEO walked in. An impressive tall man with chiseled features and black hair slicked back that had just a tinge of gray setting in at the temples, he spoke first. "Ah, our American visitors have arrived. Let me introduce myself. I am Rolfe Witig." He bowed graciously to Kristen and shook Chad's hand.

"It's a pleasure to meet you," Kristen said. "I have heard so much about your company and its history from Ms. Kroll that

I feel like I already know you. I'm Rebecca Thomas. This is my photographer, Lance Weber. We work for the *Globe*, in Boston."

"And how can I help you?" Witig asked.

Kristen went on, "I'm doing a piece for our newspaper on the multi-national pharmaceutical industry. I thought it would nice to feature Celestica since you have an American subsidiary near Boston."

"Yes. We work quite closely with our American affiliate. They may be thousands of miles away, but we are in constant communication."

"Speaking with Inger, I was impressed at your company's commitment to its workers and surrounding community here in Switzerland. Do you have similar plans in the United States?"

"As a matter of fact, yes we do. So long as a Witig is at the helm of this company, taking good care of those who work for us will be paramount. We have already established an endowment to cover scholarships for the children of those employed at our American facility."

"Do you mind?" Chad held up the camera. Witig nodded, and Chad moved around the room, taking photos of the CEO from various angles.

"Herr Witig, have you ever visited Boston?"

"Yes, on several occasions, and I was very impressed. Boston is a city steeped in both history and tradition—two things I greatly value. At the same time, the region is home to some of the world's most advanced medical institutions and innovative research."

"Herr Witig, I don't mean to touch a sensitive nerve, but I have heard that there are financial strains on your company that could affect growth of the American division. What can you tell me about that?"

"Ms. Thomas, although Celestica has recently passed through a period of fiscal challenge, we are currently investing more in our American venture than here at Geneva. We have high hopes that new products developed in the Boston area will help power our company's future growth. As a matter of fact, we have spared no expense to make the US facility a state-of-the-art operation. I believe that in a relatively short time, it will be recognized as the major arm of our international operations."

"Something special happening so close to home, that would certainly make a great angle for this article," said Kristen. "Can you tell me anything about those new products in your pipeline?"

"Well, some are still confidential, of course. But I can tell you that we are close to completing work on a new class of antibiotics that kills highly resistant strains of staphylococcus, including MRSA."

"That would be wonderful. As I mentioned to Ms. Kroll yesterday, one of my confidential sources indicated that you might also have another breakthrough soon…a product that has to do with aging?"

Celestica's CEO smiled smugly and answered, "Yes, that is quite correct. Fortunately, you arrived at precisely the right moment to be the first to hear about our revolutionary new agent. The drug is called Juvena, after Juventus, the Roman god of youth. Juvena can slow the normal aging process quite dramatically. A week from now, the data will be submitted to the European Medicines Agency, and I expect their speedy approval."

Witig continued as Kristen took copious notes. "By the way, it is not our goal to have a multitude of decrepit elderly living on forever, but rather to allow those at the peak of their productivity to maintain the energy and skills they need to remain successful. By slowing aging, we can also forestall such disabling associated illnesses as arthritis, Parkinson's, dementia, and vision or hearing loss."

"How is the treatment given? Is it a patch or perhaps a pill?"

"No. It's administered with a daily injection, like insulin for diabetics. Just one self-administered shot a day," said Witig, miming a quick injection to his arm and making a clicking noise with his tongue. "With a little shot, I can offer you the fountain of youth."

"In a injection—no thanks! I just hate needles," Kristen said, hoping her small joke would cover the shiver that went down her spine at the man's shear gall in trying to alter natures' most basic process—getting older. "Herr Witig, is it fair to say, then, that you have uncovered the secret of aging and figured out a way to control it?"

"That is precisely the case," he said, glowing with pride. "May I suggest that you both follow me into our media room?" Witig stood and was ready to lead his visitors out of his office when Chad interjected.

"Herr Witig, do you think I can take one more photo before we go? How about standing next to your grandfather?"

"Of course," Witig answered.

"Thank you. Then if you could just move over here," Chad said, pointing to the portrait of the company's elderly patriarch. Witig moved over to stand alongside the painting. Anchel Witig looked an imposing figure in the life-sized oil, sporting a large imperial mustache and monocle. A mortar and pestle, the basic tools of an apothecary, were at his side. Chad clicked off several photos. In the process, it struck him that grandson and grand-father shared one strong resemblance—the countenance of haughty arrogance.

The four rode the elevator one floor down. Witig paused briefly outside a door, preparing his guests. "The space you are about to enter has been designed to introduce Juvena to the world. What amazing luck on your part, being here today, so I can give you the first peek inside?" Witig took out his ID and waved it over a sensor. The door clicked open. The room was pitch black. "Follow me," Witig said, using a penlight to make his way, with his guests fol-lowing closely behind. "Please, stand right here." Witig continued walking and disappeared into the darkness.

A few moments later, the overhead lights slowly came on. Kristen and Chad found themselves standing in the center of a large circular auditorium, surrounded by a massive curvilinear screen. Witig stood at a podium off to one side.

"I hope you are ready to see something very special," Witig said to his guests. Then he uttered the words, "Let there be life!"

Music started to play in the background. An animated display of a human cells appeared on the screen. A distinguished baritone voice spoke as the visual sequence played. "*Watch as a Juvena liposomes merge with the cells' outer membranes and discharge their precious cargo of DNA into the interior cytoplasm.*"

On the screen, they saw scores of spherical structures melt into cell membranes. Afterward, the luminescent DNA segments from within the liposomes lit up in the interior cytoplasm. Then the DNA floated toward center of the cell and its nucleus. Chad and Kristen viewed the presentation, spellbound.

"*And now,*" continued the narrator, "*the Juvena DNA segments enters the nuclear membrane.*" The luminescent strands of DNA made their way through the membrane pores into the nucleus that contained the chromosomes. "*Watch as the Juvena DNA segments melt themselves into multiple regions on chromosome twenty-one.*" The animated chromosome on the screen lit up bright fluorescent green at multiple spots along its length. "*Those green regions correspond to promoter segments of genes involved in aging. The Juvena turns on the host of genes that keep cells young.*"

"*Juvena…the treatment that will revolutionize the way we age and the way we live.*"

With that, the show ended. Both the narration and the music stopped, and the lights came up. Witig spoke. "As you see, my friends, Juvena acts like the conductor in a symphony of cellular processes, all directed at slowing aging."

Kristen said to her host, "What a remarkable display. I've never seen anything like it. Your demonstration suggests that Celestica is definitely on the verge of achieving a huge scientific milestone."

"Thank you," Witig said, beaming. "I wholeheartedly agree with your assessment."

"When do you expect final approval for Juvena?" Kristen asked.

"Here in Europe, it should be within the next few weeks."

Chad asked, "May I take a photo with you at the podium?" At Witig's nod of consent, Chad crouched to snap a shot of Witig standing imposingly above him at the podium. Afterward, they returned to Witig's office. As she took a seat, Kristen asked the question she had been waiting to ask. "Herr Witig, do you think I could speak with the team that discovered Juvena? A brief interview with the scientists could really enhance the article."

Witig answered, "Our lead researcher on this project is a very shy and private person. He refuses to speak with the media."

Kristen went on with her pitch. "I can assure you that the impact of my piece will really be much greater if I can speak with the scientist personally."

Witig thought for a moment. "Perhaps while you have some lunch at our cafeteria, I can see if it's possible to arrange a meeting."

"That would be most kind of you, Herr Witig."

"Well, *kindness* is one of our most valued traditions at Celestica."

29

Witig went to see the man who discovered Juvena. Opening the door and walking into the lab, told its occupant, "Dr. Harris, I have very good news for you. We have decided to start letting the world know about your age defying DNA liposomes."

"Why do that now, before it is formally approved?"

"My dear doctor, you don't understand business. This is simply a matter of taking advantage when opportunity arises." Witig went on. "A reporter is here visiting from America. She is doing a story on multi-national pharmaceutical companies, and I want to make sure she focuses on Celestica. This could be worth a lot to us in free publicity. So I am *requesting* that you accommodate me by answering some questions for her during a brief interview. No negative comments, or there will be repercussions. You would not want to endanger an innocent journalist, would you?" Witig glanced over at the security guard he brought along then turned back to Harris. "You understand me, don't you?"

"You're a fucking bastard."

"Very well, Dr. Harris, I see you understand. So, put a nice smile on your face and enjoy the interview."

Inger was having lunch with the reporter and her photographer in the company cafeteria. Their meal was interrupted when her cell phone went off. It was Witig. "Please excuse me for one moment." she said, stepping away from the table to take her call.

"When you finish lunch, take them to see Harris. He should be on good behavior but stay with them during their time together to make sure."

Inger returned to her guests. "I have good news. We are about to visit, Dr. Gordon Harris, our lead scientist on the Juvena Project. Although quite reclusive, he has graciously agreed to grant you an audience. Ms. Thomas, you will be the lucky first to hear about Juvena directly from the one who discovered the cure to aging."

After lunch, Inger drove them in one of the motorized carts along the path they had followed the day before. This time, they took to turnoff to the massive building that had not been on the regular tour. Hans Spiegel, the head of on-site security, met the group outside the building to escort them inside. Inger turned to Kristen, and said "Follow me." She swiped her ID card across a sensor and the door opened automatically. They walked down a long corridor to another door that Inger opened with her key card. Inside was Gordon Harris.

Kristen and Chad prayed his response wouldn't give them away.

Inger spoke. "Dr. Harris, this is Rebecca Thomas, a reporter for the *Boston Globe*, and her photographer, Lance Weber. They are here to ask you a few questions about Juvena."

Harris kept his face impassive. He nodded coolly, but wanted to blurt out, *"Get the hell out of here!"*

"It's pleasure to meet you, Dr. Harris," Kristen said.

"Yes, well…."

"Sir, we've been told you're not inclined to be interviewed so I'm honored to be granted this rare opportunity to meet. Let me just say up front that this is very low-key, no pressure. We can stop any time you like."

"Okay, that will be fine." Harris answered. He paused and let the silence drag on. Then before anyone else could break it, he said, "Boston, huh? I worked there at one time. How is it these days?"

"The weather hasn't been the best this summer—kind of hot and muggy most of the time," Kristen answered.

"And the Red Sox, how're they doing?"

Chad answered this time. "They're in second place, and on a winning streak. If they keep it up, who knows? It could mean the pennant."

"That's music to my ears," Harris said grinning.

"So, sir, how long have you been with Celestica?"

"I've been working for them a little over a year."

"What are the conditions like doing your research here in Switzerland?"

"I have all the latest equipment at my disposal," said Harris. "And the company is very supportive of my work."

"What do you think of the company CEO, Herr Witig?"

"Rolfe Witig? He is a man of unusual vision who makes a point of meeting with me regularly to discuss my project. You might say he keeps me on task."

Inger smiled, listening to Harris's surprising accolades of her boss.

Kristen continued, "Dr. Harris, I understand that you have developed a treatment that slows the aging process, a 'fountain-of-youth' drug, so to speak."

"Well, I have been working with a DNA liposome that was originally intended as treatment of children with the rare disorder of accelerated aging, progeria. However, the drug also considerably slows down aging in normal individuals. Celestica has decided to broaden the treatment's application and offer it to the general public." He turned to Inger and said, "I think it's fair to say that, don't you?"

Inger could feel her face turning red. She defended the company's decision. "May I clarify?" she said. "Celestica wants people to have an opportunity to avoid the disabling maladies of old age—arthritis, senility, macular degeneration, immobility—for as long as possible."

"That seems quite reasonable," Kristen agreed, in an effort to appease her. "Perhaps this would be a good time for Lance to take some pictures. Is that all right, Dr. Harris? Just tell him if there's anything confidential he can't show in a photo."

"Of course," Harris answered. "It's good to hear a familiar accent. I feel like I'm among old friends."

Chad almost choked at Harris's comment, but instead began methodically setting up the umbrella reflector and the tripod. He took several shots of Harris alone, with his research mice, and next to his whiteboard covered in complex biochemical equations. Then Chad called over to his host. "Ms. Kroll, please stand over here and let me take your picture with Dr. Harris."

Not able to resist an opportunity for recognition, Inger agreed. She took a compact from her purse to look at herself and adjusted her hair. She put on a fresh coat of lipstick, then set her purse on a table and walked over to Harris. Kristen noticed an ID badge sticking out from her purse. While Inger had her back turned, Kristen eased the ID out of the purse and stuffed it inside Chad's camera bag.

After pictures were taken, Kristen bid Harris goodbye. "Thank you, Dr. Harris, for granting this interview. I know how much you value your privacy, so I appreciate all the more you speaking about your remarkable discovery."

"Ms. Thomas, you are entirely welcome. The pleasure was all mine."

Chad shook hands with Harris, "I don't know much about science but your discovery sounds pretty spectacular."

Harris smiled. "Why, thank you, Lance. That's very kind to say. Ms. Thomas, please be sure to send me a copy of your article once it is published. I very much look forward to reading it."

When they were riding back to the administrative building in the cart, Inger asked, "Did you find your time here at Celestica informative?"

"Very much so," Kristen answered. "I have more than enough info to write about Celestica. Please thank Herr Witig once again for his hospitality. I really appreciate his seeing us on such short notice."

"I shall," Inger assured her visitors. With that, Chad and Kristen got into their rental car and left the facility.

**

Back in her office, Inger immediately phoned Witig. "I couldn't be happier," she told him. "The interview with Harris went off like a charm. He spoke so positively about the company, I wasn't sure the words were actually coming from his lips."

"Excellent," Witig responded. "Harris has *finally* learned to cooperate, or at least to avoid what would happen if he doesn't."

"Now, let's get on to a topic of *real* importance," Inger suggested.

"What would that be?"

"Where shall I make dinner reservations in Paris for when we arrive to celebrate the agency approval?"

"Hmm…" Witig tried to recall the name of the restaurant his ex-wife incessantly boasted about after her shopping trip to Paris. When it popped into his head he said, "Perhaps Le Grand Véfour?"

Inger answered, "Your wish is my command."

30

Murdock, whose team was frantically searching Boston for Reynolds and his girlfriend, decided to do something stupidly simple. He called Boston General and asked the operator to page Dr. Reynolds. "Sir," the operator said, "The doctor is unavailable. His calls are being referred to his office. Shall I connect you?"

"Yes, please."

The operator transferred his call to Chad's office. Miriam answered. "Can I help you?" she asked.

"I'd like to schedule an appointment for my son to see Dr. Reynolds."

"I am so sorry, but Dr. Reynolds will be unavailable for appointments for the next week, although he will be calling in."

"What do you mean?"

"Oh, a last-minute situation came up and he had to leave for a conference abroad."

"Abroad...I see," Murdock said. "Well, I'll call back after he returns. It's not an emergency."

"Thank you for your understanding."

When he got off the phone Murdock was furious. *What the hell is Reynolds up to?*

Next he called over to the *Globe* and asked for Kristen Ross. "I'm looking for Ms. Ross. I have some information on a story she is doing."

"Oh, can I take a message? Kristen is out of town right now, but she should be back in a few days."

"Any idea where she went so I might try to reach her?"

"No, but can I take a message?"

"Don't bother. I'll call back next week."

Murdock slammed the receiver down. Suddenly it all made sense. He screamed, "God damn!" Picking a paperweight off the desk, Murdock threw it full force against the wall. *How could I have been so dumb not to realize where they were?*

✶✶

It was getting dark when Chad drove the car back up to the front gate of the Celestica facility. He spoke to the guard who had let them in earlier that day. "I'm sorry, but I forgot one of my camera lenses during our photo shoot with Herr Witig. I just need to pick it up."

"Sure, no problem," said the guard. He pressed a button and the gate opened, allowing their car to proceed. Instead of stopping at the administrative building, Chad headed to the building where they met Harris.

Kristen used Inger's ID card to enter the building. They ran down the hall to the lab where they had interviewed Harris. They hurried inside, surprised that the lab door wasn't locked. Soon they knew why: Harris wasn't there.

Chad turned to Kristen. "Where the heck is he?" They looked around the room and saw lab equipment, a desk, and a computer. "No bed," Chad said, thinking out loud. "They must take him somewhere else to sleep…. but where?" He scanned the facility layout on the map and noticed a smaller building close to where they were located. "If I had to park Harris somewhere for the night, this is where I'd put him, as close to where he works as possible."

"Well, let's get going," Kristen suggested. They rushed outside and ran down a path toward the building Chad spotted on their map.

**

"Look, I know where Harris's doctor friend and the girl are," Murdock told Anderson. "They went to Switzerland."

"What!"

"Yes, I'm guessing those two troublemakers left Boston to try to find Harris and bring him back."

Anderson growled at Murdock, "Well, get your ass over to Geneva and find them before they manage to screw up our whole operation. I'll call Witig and let him know what's happening."

**

Chad and Kristen found the building they were looking for. Only one room at a far end on the ground floor had a light showing. They headed over toward the window with the light but it was too high to look into. "Kristen, climb up," Chad suggested, cupping his hands so she could step on and be high enough to see inside. Peering through, Kristen saw Harris sitting on a cot, reading. She tapped on the window. Harris looked up, saw her, and ran over.

"What are you doing here? They'll kill you."

"We came to get you out, Dr. Harris. Grab what you need and meet us at the main door. I have an access card."

"But...I'm not locked in."

"Not locked in? Then get out here now!"

A few moments later Harris was standing alongside his friends. "I can't believe you weren't locked in," Kristen said.

Harris didn't respond to her observation. Instead he asked, "Do you have any idea the kind of the trouble you two are in? There are security cameras everywhere. And these are cold-blooded killers you're dealing with."

Chad answered, "They would have killed us if we stayed in Boston, so we thought as an alternative, why not visit Switzerland?"

"This is no time for joking." Harris angrily retorted.

"You're right," Chad answered. "Let's go and get the hell out of here."

**

Anderson's phone call caught Witig just as he was ready to leave his office for the evening. "I've just put Murdock on the company jet to Switzerland."

"Oh? How nice of you to allow him such an expensive vacation on the company tab."

"It's no vacation Herr Witig. Harris's colleague, Chad Reynolds, and his girlfriend, Kristen Ross, a reporter for the *Boston Globe*, are over there somewhere, probably trying to find some way to get Harris out as we speak.

"Dammit!" Witig hollered. "Reporters…it must have been them here. They were in my office. The woman knew about Juvena, and she asked me all kinds of questions. I told her about our anti-aging treatment, thinking it was a real interview. I even let her speak with Harris." Witig's face twisted in anger. "And that fucking photographer had the audacity to take a picture of me alongside my grandfather's portrait!"

"Look, I suggest you immediately put an around-the-clock watch on Harris. If you happen to capture Reynolds and Ross, hold them for Murdock. He'll know what to do."

Witig realized that the entire Juvena project was in jeopardy. And it was not just Juvena, but the future of his company on the line. He felt a dull throbbing sensation begin in his head and, knowing that the pain would come soon, he reached into his drawer and took out a dose of pain-killer. Next, Witig picked up the phone and called his chief of on-site security, Hans Spiegel. "Hans, I need you to check on Harris right away. Keep a close eye on him. I have just received word from Anderson that two of his old friends from Boston may try to steal him away."

"No problem, Herr Witig. I will go immediately. But if I may, can I ask why would Harris leave when he knows that he will die within days if he does?"

"Just check on him. The man is unpredictable. By the way, Murdock is on his way from Boston to help with disposing of our unwanted visitors once we catch them."

31

"Where are we going?" Harris asked, breathless, as he tried hard to keep up with Chad and Kristen's pace. "Can you slow down a little? Chad encouraged his friend, "Our car is parked right in front of your lab building. It's not much farther. Come on, you can do it."

As they continued up the path, a light appeared around a corner. Two glowing orbs sped toward them—Hans Spiegel, riding in a motorized cart. Kristen and Chad stopped and backed up into the shadows as the vehicle approached, halting just in front of Harris. Spiegel climbed down and stood next to him. A gun glinted in his hand.

"Dr. Harris, you know you're not supposed to be out of your room," said Spiegel. "Are you alone? I thought I heard you talking to someone."

"No, it's just me and I-I'm…not feeling well…" Harris stumbled and fell forward, toward the backlit figure. Spiegel instinctively held both arms out to catch him and as he did, Kristen sprang forward kicking at the one holding his gun. The sound of the guard's bone snapping was audible. He fell to his knees, holding his arm and groaning in agony.

Kristen's next kick went to the man's chest, throwing him backward onto the ground. Chad picked up the weapon, which turned out to be a Taser. Harris saw the guard suddenly reach with his good arm for a knife strapped to his lower leg.

"Look out!" Harris warned. "He's going for a knife."

A jolt of electricity emitted by the Taser wires sent the guard's body into spasms. His face became hideously contorted and the sudden contraction of his chest muscles forced the air out of his lungs, producing an inhuman howl. Hans lay incapacitated on the ground. Chad took the guard's handcuffs and put them around his wrists, then removed the guard's belt to bind his legs.

Chad turned to Kristen, "That was pretty impressive, even for you."

"All those trophies you complain are cluttering our apartment? I didn't get them for nothing."

"Well, I'll never complain about them again. How about helping me lug this bum out of sight?" Kristen and Chad dragged Spiegel well off the path. By the time anyone found him, they would be long gone. Chad flung the guard's knife into the woods, but stuffed the Taser into his pocket.

They finally made it to their car. Chad drove with the lights off down the road toward the front gate. There they found the guard standing in the middle of the road with his hand up, blocking their exit. He motioned for them to slow down and stop, but Chad had no intention of obeying. Instead, he gunned the car, forcing the man to jump backward just before ramming the Peugeot through the exit gate. The guard who had greeted them so cordially when they entered returned to a gateless driveway, furiously cursing after them.

"What's he saying Kristen?" Chad asked.

"I think something not very nice about your mother."

Nervous laughter erupted inside the car as it sped away. A few miles down the road, Harris said, "You know something—it feels good to be free again. What are you planning to do now?"

"Well," Chad answered, "I suppose we go back to our hotel and wait. There's a flight back to Boston tomorrow morning."

Harris said, "I don't think that's very wise. The hotel will probably be the first place they go looking for us."

"But I have to go back. I'm not going to part with my laptop, and I left it in the room," said Kristen. "It's got all my work files."

Chad looked at her "But, Kris—"

"Don't but me! I'll go back by myself if I have to," she said, determined. Thirty minutes later, they were at the hotel. As a compromise, Kristen agreed that Chad would be the one to go inside and retrieve her computer while she stayed behind with Harris. He tucked the guard's Taser under his belt, pulled his shirt out to cover it, and left the car. When Chad reached their room, he saw the message light blinking on the phone. Chad grabbed Kristen's computer and shoved it into a backpack along with her notes, then scooped up everything else of theirs he could carry.

Before leaving, he quickly listened to the recorded message. It was Inger Kroll. "Herr Witig very much enjoyed meeting you. Have a pleasant trip back to the States. We look forward to reading your article about our company." Chad grinned but his expression soon transformed to one of apprehension. *They knew where we were staying.*

**

The security guard at Celestica's front gate tried to reach his superior, Hans Spiegel. He called several times by walkie-talkie and got no response, so he left his post to look for him. It didn't take the guard long to find Spiegel, who was calling for help while struggling in the underbrush to free himself.

"Get these fucking things off me," Spiegel ordered. "The key is in my left shirt pocket." When his colleague began to remove the cuffs, Spiegel screamed in pain. "Be careful, you idiot. My arm is broken."

"What happened?" the guard asked, bewildered, as he helped his boss up.

"Never mind that now," Spiegel snapped. "Why did you leave your post?"

"The Americans drove their car through the front gate, almost running me over. They had someone else in the car with them. I tried to reach you on the walkie-talkie, but got no answer, so I left to find you."

"Well, I'm glad you did," Spiegel told him. "Unfortunately, I've got to do something now that will be even more painful than my broken arm.

"What's that?"

"Call Witig, and tell him that Harris and the Americans got away."

**

Murdock was flying in style on the company jet, unaware of the events transpiring at the Geneva headquarters. He knew the background of his counterpart, Hans Spiegel, the security head for Celestica in Switzerland. Spiegel had once been a member of the Vatican's Swiss Guard. On the surface, in official uniform, the Swiss Guard looked like they belonged in a museum; in reality, each had skills comparable to the most elite modern military force anywhere. Between the two of them, Murdock was confident that Harris, Reynolds, and Ross would soon be rounded up. As he finished his cocktail at thirty-five thousand feet over the Atlantic and prepared to nap, a call came in by satellite phone. It was Witig. "Thank God you are on your way here," he said.

"Why is that?" Murdock asked.

"Harris's two friends from Boston have just taken him from our complex."

"Shit," Murdock said. "Where the hell was Hans when this was happening?"

"He was right there but somehow they got hold of his Taser and turned it on him. One of them broke his arm."

"I'll bet it was the woman. That bitch is something else," Murdock said. "She put one of my men in the hospital with a broken leg. I'll have to give Ms. Ross special attention when I find her. She'll beg me to kill her before I'm through."

Witig said, "You need to find them quickly. And when you do, don't waste any time. Dispose of them all."

Murdock wanted to make sure he heard right. "Including Dr. Harris?"

"Yes. He's not essential any more. I have all the data for the regulatory panel to approve his drug, regardless of whether he's dead or alive. And now we also have his mice for a demonstration." Witig went on. "I can get any one of a dozen other scientists to appear in Harris's place."

"But why do you think he left? Harris must realize he's committing suicide."

"I can't answer that, since he knows what will happen without his daily injection of Juvena. I suppose it was stupid of us, but we didn't even bother locking him into his room anymore because we knew Harris understood that he would die a miserable death without the shots if he ran away. Apparently his own life doesn't matter to him anymore."

"Good thing for us that he's a dead man, no matter what," Murdock correctly deduced.

"When you catch them, if Harris is still alive, try to make his death look accidental. At least that will give us some additional free publicity: 'Life of world famous geneticist who discovered Juvena, a cure for aging, cut short by tragic accident.'"

Murdock glanced at his watch. "I'll be landing in about three hours," he told Witig. "In the meantime, have your people search the city and see if they can locate them. Is Spiegel able help out?"

"I'm sure Hans will try even if he has to take a whole bottle of pain killer to do it."

"Good. The poor guy should have the satisfaction of being there when I catch them and make them suffer…before they die."

**

The trio was not sure where they could spend the night safely before their flight to the United States the next day. They had little doubt that they would be hunted. "What if we go to the police?" Kristen proposed.

Harris said, "With all money and influence the Witig family has around here, there's too much of a chance we could get double-crossed."

"I agree," Chad chimed in. "We'd better think of something else."

"What about another hotel?" Kristen asked.

"They'll be checking hotels all over Geneva for us," Chad answered. "They could probably cover every one of them in a matter of hours." He thought for a moment then asked, "Kristen, what do you think about going back to that place we had dinner last night, Le Château? It had guest rooms."

"I suppose that might work. It's outside the city, and known mainly as a restaurant, not a hotel. They might not expect us to return there." A few minutes later, Chad took an exit off the autobahn and headed down a road toward Le Château.

**

Spiegel picked Murdock up at the airport, his broken arm in a cast. Once his American cohort was inside the car, he handed him a .22 caliber pistol and silencer. "You will need this," he said. Murdock smiled and took the weapon. "Hans, do you want me to drive? Murdock asked, pointing to Spiegel's arm cast.

"Sure, you take the wheel. I'll tell you where to go."

From the airport they drove directly to the hotel in Geneva where the Americans had checked in. The driver kept the car idling at the hotel's rear. Spiegel stopped by the front desk with Murdock. "May I speak with Franco?" Spiegel asked. He knew Franco Orsi, the hotel's manager. Celestica occasionally had guests stay at his hotel while they were negotiating business. On more than one occasion, Spiegel had paid Orsi a bonus for special extras to satisfy Celestica guests' needs, like female companionship or drugs.

"Hans, it's so good to see you," Orsi said, coming out of the back room. "How can I help you?"

"Franco, I need a small favor. Tell me which room is registered under the name Rebecca Thomas."

"One moment, please." Orsi went the computer and studied the screen. "Looks like room 532."

"I need an access key."

"No problem," Franco said. He took a blank key card ran it though the programmer, then handed it to Hans.

"And this is a little something for your trouble," Spiegel said, passing Franco an envelope filled with money.

"You are too kind," Orsi said, bowing courteously. "What happened to your arm?"

"I slipped in the shower." Spiegel answered curtly.

"Sorry to hear that," Orsi said. "I have only one request." The manager asked politely, "Please, don't make too much of a mess? Getting bloodstains out of carpeting is a real bitch."

"Don't worry, Franco. I'll do my best and pay for any cleanup that's necessary."

Spiegel led Murdock to a stairwell. When they reached the fifth floor, they walked down the hall to room 532, guns drawn. A shot with the small caliber bullet could kill without causing the mess Franco feared since it wouldn't produce an exit wound.

Spiegel used the key card Franco gave him then cautiously pushed the door open. The entryway was dark. Reynolds and Ross would be dead before they opened their eyes. Murdock carried a syringe filled with sedative for Harris; he needed to set up a phony accident for him, as Witig requested. Spiegel and Murdock looked at each other, then Murdock gave a hand signal to enter the bedroom.

"Fuck it!" Murdock exclaimed a moment later, flipping the light switch on. "They're gone!"

32

The staff at Le Château rushed to attend the VIP couple arriving. Witig was grateful for their attention; it had been a long and trying day. The charade by the American reporter that led to Harris's escape had left him unsettled. He needed a distraction, and what better place than Le Château? The food and accommodations were superb, and its personnel completely discreet.

While a bellman carried in their luggage, Witig and Inger headed directly to the restaurant. "Thank you, Herr Witig, for joining us this evening," the maître d' said as he led Witig and Inger to their favorite table, which had a spectacular view of the lake and mountains. A few minutes later, the chef made a personal appearance at their table. "How fortunate, Herr Witig, you came to dine with us tonight. I made a special trip early this morning and personally selected the absolutely best truffles at the market. I have used them in some wonderful preparations for our menu tonight."

"Henri, you are my culinary god," Witig said, slipping the chef a large-denomination bill with his handshake.

After their sumptuous meal, arm in arm and giddy from wine, Witig and Inger approached the front desk to pick up their room key. The manager, Kurt, was behind the counter. "Herr Witig and Madame! What a pleasure that you are joining us this evening. Your suite is ready and waiting. And may I also take this opportunity to thank you for sending us the Americans as guests."

"I'm sorry. I don't understand," Witig answered, confused.

"They dined here last night," said Inger. "I sent them." She scowled.

"Yes, they were here last evening for dinner. But they returned tonight, and brought along a friend. They are spending the night with us."

Smiling, Inger turned to the manager. "Kurt, I'm sure they now love Le Château's exquisite ambiance as much as we do. They came all the way from America to interview Herr Witig. Naturally, I recommended them to the best hotelier I know."

"Thank you, Madame," Kurt said, bowing graciously.

Witig thought, *My God, Hans is looking for them all over Geneva, and they're staying right here, all three of them. What luck!*

Then he announced, "Ach, my cell phone is vibrating. Please excuse me while I answer." Witig walked away from the counter, pretending to take a call. When he returned, he had a disappointed look on his face. "Bad news, an emergency has come up. Unfortunately, this must take precedence. Madame and I must head back as soon as possible."

"I'm sorry to hear that, Herr Witig. Perhaps we might be fortunate enough to have you return later this week."

"Perhaps," Witig answered, pivoting to lead Inger out the door. Soon a bellman rushed after them with the luggage that was never unpacked.

Inger was visibly upset. Inside the car, she glared at Rolfe. "What are you doing? I thought we were going to enjoy ourselves tonight. We deserve it, after today."

"Inger, please, now is not the time to complain. It wouldn't be wise for us to stay tonight considering…what will happen later on. It could lead to questioning. I will phone Hans immediately to let him know that the people he's looking for are here." Witig turned to Inger with a diabolical grin. "It will be the last night the three of them spend alive."

✳✳

Chad estimated a thirty-minute drive on the autobahn from Le Château to Genève Aéroport. Their flight home was scheduled to take off at noon the next day. However, with such ruthless people looking for them, it wouldn't make for a very peaceful night, even in the secluded luxury of Le Château.

Chad phoned Boston General and spoke to Miriam. "I'll be back at work day after tomorrow. Please let Dr. Warner know, because he's been covering me. Before we hang up, though, there's someone here who wants to speak with you."

"Miriam, it's me, Gordon." The familiar voice took her breath away.

"Oh, gosh, Dr. Harris, it's so good to hear from you!"

"Well, I'm very much looking forward to seeing you again, and soon."

"You're coming back?"

"Well, I'd like to, but first I need your help. Can you find my passport and fax a copy to the hotel where I'm staying?"

"Sure. I'll have to do a little digging through your things in storage, but I'm sure I can find it," she said. "But wait…I thought you took a job overseas last year. Didn't you need your passport for that?"

"It's a long story," said Harris. "And one I'll save for later. Thanks, Miriam. You're the best. You were always the best."

"Oh, you're making me blush, Dr. Harris. Just hurry back, I can't wait."

"If all goes well I will be there in person day after tomorrow." He read Miriam a number for the fax in their room.

She told him excitedly, "You know, Dr. Harris, I've been waiting for this phone call over a year! Your passport info will be arriving shortly." Then she hung up.

Kristen was thinking out loud. "I'm not sure about staying here all night. Maybe the airport is the safest place to go. There were police were all over the terminal when we arrived." She continued. "It's unlikely anyone would try to harm us once we're there. It's getting to the airport that might be difficult."

"Look, we're all tired. Let's try to get some rest now and leave early. We'll take shifts staying up tonight, just in case," Chad suggested.

For a while, they watched television, reminisced about old times, and made small talk. Chad said, "I have a confession to make. I really enjoyed playing the photographer. When I get back to Boston, I might take some classes and see if I can get good at it."

"I have a small confession to make as well," said Kristen. "Chad, when you weren't looking, I ate a bar of incredibly delicious Swiss chocolate. Sorry, I didn't offer to share. Will you ever forgive me?"

"I think I can give you absolution for that sin," Chad answered. While the couple was joking around, Harris remained silent. "Gordon, you're so quiet. No confessions to share? What's on your mind?"

"Oh, yes," Harris said, hesitating as if his thoughts were elsewhere. Halfheartedly he said, "I...I confess that I really don't really care if the Red Sox take the American league pennant."

In fact, Harris didn't have the heart to tell them what he was really thinking. *Without continuing the Juvena injections, I have only about forty-eight hours left to live.*

**

Murdock drove the black Mercedes into the parking lot of Le Château. Spiegel sat in the passenger seat, his broken arm casted and in a sling. "That's their rental car," he said, pointing to the plate number that matched the one given by the guard from Celestica's gatehouse.

"No doubt about it. The front end has damage from ramming the gate when they made their getaway," said Spiegel. "I'd love to go in right now and shoot them all!"

"Be patient, my friend," Murdock cautioned. "Le Château is a small, intimate place. You'd be recognized immediately. And remember, Witig wants Harris's death to look like an accident."

"So, what's the plan?"

"They will unquestionably go straight to the airport from here," said Murdock. "They'll take the autobahn. We'll follow them. On the way, we can eliminate all of them at once, and it will appear that all three died in a regrettable accident." The two security men circled the lot then parked at the end. All they had to do now was wait and watch.

**

At six in the morning, the three Americans emerged from Le Château and got into their rented Peugeot. The sun was just rising over the Alps to the east, sending rays of light dancing across Lac Léman. Chad started the car and began the drive to the airport. Harris sat in the passenger seat and Kristen in the back.

"Look, how nice," Murdock said sarcastically as the rental pulled out of the lot. "They're all wearing seatbelts. I think they'll need more than that to stay alive."

The early Sunday morning traffic was light on the autobahn. The Peugeot's occupants chatted nervously, all of them on edge after a sleepless night. Chad checked his mirrors obsessively. As they drove on, Chad noticed a black Mercedes approaching rapidly in the rearview mirror. He was in the middle lane, and the black car had plenty of room to pass by, but it continued to come up behind. Chad sped up, but the car continued to gain on them. Soon it was close enough for Chad to make out a menacing-looking driver and his passenger, a man with his arm in a cast.

"Hold on everybody," he said, knowing what was coming next. The Mercedes rammed the Peugeot hard from behind.

"What was that?" Kristen gasped, whipping her head around to look. The Mercedes fell back half a car length, but kept pace with the Peugeot. Chad looked in the rearview mirror again. The man driving was laughing. A few seconds later, another jolt came from behind. "What the hell!" Kristen exclaimed. "The driver must be out of his mind!"

The Mercedes pulled into the inside lane and drove next to the rental. It swerved abruptly toward the Peugeot, stopping short of making contact. Harris looked into the Mercedes—Murdock and Spiegel! The tiny Peugeot was no match for the larger, more powerful German sedan. Chad had the gas pedal pressed to the floor, and still could not pull away from the Mercedes.

The window of the Mercedes lowered, and Murdock signaled for Harris to open his window. He shouted across, "Harris, you've been a big pain in my ass. But now you fucking lose and I win! I wanted to tell you that before you die." A moment later, Murdock rammed hard into the Peugeot's side and sent it lurching into the passing lane. Any harder and the collision would have thrown them off the highway into a concrete median. He again slammed the rental on the passenger side. This time Peugeot hit the median then luckily bounced back into the passing lane.

Kristen screamed, "He's going to kill us!" Both cars were driving neck to neck at top speed down the autobahn. Harris could see Murdock laughing, and realized he was toying with them. Murdock could have eliminated them quickly and easily already, but this was too much fun for him. The fiend was taking perverse pleasure in their terror before going in for the final kill.

Harris blurted out, "Chad, give me the Taser!" He lowered his window then called out to Murdock. "I just want *you* to know that this is for Todd and Claire!" Harris saw the confused look on Murdock's face as he lifted the Taser and took aim. For a split second, Murdock realized what was about to happen, but had no time to respond. The Taser wires shot out and caught him on the neck. As its fifty thousand volts of electricity surged, Murdock's body was sent into uncontrollable spasms. The speeding

Mercedes suddenly careened to the right while Spiegel, in the passenger seat, desperately tried to reach over and control the steering wheel with his one good arm.

The Mercedes fishtailed wildly, drove up the low end of a guardrail and rolled over several times. Kristen had the best view from the back seat. She watched the black car skid down the road on its crushed roof, sending sparks flying, then remarked, "I hope they were wearing their seatbelts."

Minutes later, they reached the airport exit. "I think we'll skip the car rental return," said Chad. "It's time to get the hell out of Switzerland." No one disagreed.

**

An ambulance rushed to the site of an unusual single-car accident on the autobahn. The paramedics needed special equipment to extract the two men inside the tangled wreckage of the Mercedes. Thanks to the car's airbags, which had deployed from every direction, the occupants were still alive. While on their way to the closest hospital, the ambulance crew speculated on what might have caused the Mercedes to crash and concluded it must have been a blowout, or some unusual mechanical failure. "No car is perfect, not even a Mercedes." None of the medics had noticed two puncture marks on the driver's neck, left by the Taser prongs.

Murdock went into shock soon after arrival at the emergency room, then deteriorated into cardiac arrest. Using a defibrillator, doctors eventually got a rhythm back, and he survived, but was left with brain damage. Weeks later, the patient was transferred from the hospital to a nursing home with a feeding tube and on a respirator. William Murdock would remain there in a vegetative state for the rest of his shortened life.

Hans Spiegel, who already had a broken arm before the crash, suffered a compound fracture of his left femur and tibia. After extensive surgery, the orthopedic surgeon told him he was lucky to still have his reconstructed leg and that one day, with enough rehab, he might be able to walk again using a cane. From his hospital bed Spiegel filled out papers for permanent disability with his employer, Celestica Pharmaceutical.

33

Although shaken by the events on the autobahn, once the trio drove into the airport they felt relieved. Leaving the damaged Peugeot in the long-term parking lot, they headed for Swissair check in. Harris wiped off the Taser, wrapped it in a piece of newspaper, then threw in a trash bin before they entered the terminal.

On their way to the gate, Kristen suddenly exclaimed to her compatriots, "Oh, gosh! I just remembered something. Go on ahead. I'll meet up with you in a minute." Running back to a kiosk they had passed, it didn't take long to find what she wanted.

When she returned, Chad and Harris met her with quizzical stares. "Is everything okay?" Chad asked. She nodded reassuringly.

On the jet, Kristen took out her computer and started typing away. "What are you doing?" Chad asked.

"I'm writing the article about Celestica, while things are still fresh in my mind."

Chad turned to Harris, "By the way, I've got Flower's confession about Murdock arranging for the dead girl's overdose on tape. I think that should be enough to clear you."

"What about Juvena and my patients with progeria? I was forced to sign over the rights to Celestica."

"We'll find a good lawyer to go after them."

"I'm a doctor," Harris said. "I have an allergy to lawyers." They laughed.

Sunset came, then darkness as they flew toward Boston. Chad and Harris fell asleep, while Kristen feverishly typed away on her laptop.

34

Soon after landing, Kristen and Chad headed to the *Globe* headquarters. She entered her editor's office. Kristen had emailed him the completed article about Celestica from the plane, just to be safe, but now she placed a jump drive containing her work and Chad's photos onto his desk. "Rodney, I think you'll like what's on this. Please don't wait a week to start reading it—this damn story nearly cost me my life."

Her editor looked at her with consternation. "Yeah, yeah, that's what they all say. Everyone expects me to drop what I'm doing when they put something on my desk." He looked up at Kristen. She was not laughing.

"I am not exaggerating. Trust me," she said. "And to show how much I love you, I brought back something special." Kristen produced a box of Teuscher Swiss chocolate, the item she ran back to buy from a kiosk at the Geneva airport terminal before departing.

"Say, Kristen, this is really nice. How did you know I have a weakness for this stuff?"

"I have my sources. Anyway, consider it an incentive to read my article *now*."

"To tell you the truth, Kristen, I'm totally swamped." He paused, then holding up the box of chocolate said, "But for this...I'll try my best."

"Rodney, you won't regret it. This is a *big* story. Front page big."

While Kristen was talking to her editor, Chad was returning the borrowed photography equipment to the real Lance Weber's office. "Is everything still working?" asked Lance.

"I'm happy to say, yes. And I enjoyed being *you* for a few days." Chad laid the press ID badge that Lance doctored with Chad's photo down on his desk.

Lance let out a sigh of relief. "Get any good shots?"

"You tell me," Chad answered. "I downloaded copies onto my flash drive, but I left the originals on the camera for backup. It's important stuff, though it may not look like it yet."

Lance downloaded the digital files to his computer then reviewed the photos in slideshow format. "Hey, these are not too shabby for an amateur. Chad, I think you definitely have a good eye for composition."

"Thanks. Truth is, I enjoyed myself so much that I've decided to take it up as a serious hobby."

Lance thought for a moment then said, "Hang on a minute." Heading for a closet, he made noise rummaging through the clutter and returned with a camera in hand. "Here, I want you to have this. It's an older Leica, but it still takes amazing pictures. Consider it a gift from me to a budding photographer."

Chad was floored. "I don't know what to say. This is fantastic."

"Use it and have fun. The camera doesn't do any good sitting on a shelf."

"I promise to put it to good use."

"And feel free to stop by anytime. I'd be happy to give you a few pointers." They shook hands, then Chad left Lance's office to join up with Kristen, proudly carrying his new camera.

**

Later that day, Chad met with Harris. "I think it's time we go to the police," Chad said. "I've got the audio confession of Flowers." He held up the recording for Harris to see. "It's a shame we don't have the digital photo chip, too."

"Who says?" Taking off one of his shoes, Harris pulled something from under the insole. Holding up the memory chip, he said, "I'm not proud of what's on this, but since these pictures strengthen the case against Celestica, we'll take it along."

Chad was shocked. "Jesus, Gordon, how the heck did you manage to hold onto that?"

"It's been in my shoe since the night you gave it to me at the Yankee Clipper." Harris continued telling his surprised friend. "When I went to use the restroom, I stuck it under my insole for safekeeping."

**

At the precinct, Lieutenant Monroe took their individual statements. After that, they all met in a conference room. Monroe read through a draft of Kristen's story; which her editor had green-lighted to headline in the Globe's Sunday edition.

"Dr. Harris, it seems like you've been through one hell of an ordeal. All I can say is that Boston's finest will do its best to make sure those responsible are held accountable for these crimes." The lieutenant continued. "I'm putting several of my top detectives on your case, and I will personally liaison with the district attorney. She will decide how best to proceed with charges against Celestica and the people who held you."

"Thank you," Harris said.

"You can leave now, but let me know the best way to get in touch if I need to."

Kristen handed the officer her *Globe* business card. Chad and Harris looked at each other, and Chad answered for both of them. "Officer Monroe, it's not hard to find us. Just call Boston General and have us paged."

Officer Monroe hit himself on the forehead with his palm. "Duh!" Everyone in the room laughed.

Walking down the steps leading out of the police station, Harris was ecstatic. His friends were safe and it looked like the evildoers at Celestica would be held accountable for their crimes. However, by the time they returned to Chad's apartment, Harris wasn't feeling well.

Chad noticed that his friend looked flushed. "Are you all right?"

"I'll be fine. I'm just beat," said Harris. "Why don't you and Kristen go out for a nice dinner together? You both deserve it. Go celebrate this day on my behalf."

Chad didn't argue. Although he didn't like leaving Harris alone, not knowing whether their might have other Celestica operatives still working in the area, he thought Harris could use the rest after the tumultuous past few days.

When the two returned to the apartment after dinner, they didn't see Harris. The door to the bathroom was closed, and they heard water running, so they figured he was inside. As time passed and Harris didn't appear, they grew worried. Chad knocked on the door. "Gordon, are you okay?" There was no answer. When he forced the door open, Chad found him sprawled on the tiled floor wearing only his boxers. His eyes were glazed, and he was covered with perspiration. Chad bent down to feel for a pulse. Harris was burning up with fever. He called out, "Kristen, call 911!"

Chad shook Harris and called his name, but he only groaned. While putting cold wet towels over his friend, Chad noticed the injection marks all over Harris's thighs and realized at once what had happened: as insurance, so Harris wouldn't try to escape from Celestica, he had been given daily Juvena injections. Running away would be tantamount to signing his death sentence. But why hadn't Harris said anything about receiving the injections?

When the paramedics arrived, they took a set of vitals; Harris's temperature was already 104 degrees. Chad rode in the ambulance alongside his critically ill mentor. By the time they hit the ER, Harris was in deep coma. His temperature was 106 degrees. If his fever didn't come down soon, he would die from hyperthermia. The emergency room personnel packed him in ice, but his temperature didn't budge. Something else had to be done.

Chad picked up the hospital phone and put in an urgent page in for one of the cardiac surgeons, Marc Creager. "Hey, Marc, it's Chad Reynolds. I need your help right away."

"What's up?" Marc asked, hearing the urgency in Chad's voice.

"I'm in the emergency room with a very sick friend."

"Heart attack?"

"No, but I need you here just the same."

When Creager saw the comatose patient surrounded by bags of ice, he was shocked. "Gordon Harris!" he shouted. "Wow! I took my pediatric rotation with him ages ago when I was a resident."

"Yes," Chad said. "And now he's got severe hyperthermia that isn't responding to icing. Can you try putting him on a bypass machine and cooling him down that way? It might buy me some time so I can treat what's causing this."

"If you think it will help, of course." Creager made a few phone calls, and within minutes had mobilized his cardiac team. Harris was moved to the surgical ICU, where Creager inserted tubing into Harris's leg vein and artery, then connected it to a bypass machine like he used for patients during open-heart surgery. Once Harris's blood was circulating through the machine, its powerful cooling mechanism began lowering his body temperature.

Chad ran from the surgical ICU to the research building. He went into his office and headed for the locked refrigerator, where he plugged in the access code and searched inside. *Yes!* The vials of Juvena were still on the shelf. Chad guessed at the proper dosage for a human, drew it up into a syringe and ran back to ICU. He gave Harris the injection then repeated giving him a dose every three hours, hoping the hyperthermic withdrawal reaction could be controlled the same way it had been with the sick mice. Chad remained with his friend throughout the stormy night, dozing in a chair at his bedside.

By morning, Harris's eyes opened. He couldn't move because he was tied down with restraints and still connected to the bypass machine. "What the hell have you done to me?" Harris croaked through parched lips.

"I just tried to save your life, that's all." Chad answered, holding a glass of water up for his friend and guiding the straw into his mouth. "Why in heaven's name didn't you tell me they were giving you Juvena injections to keep you put?"

"If I'd told you that in Switzerland, you might've tried to go back and get some Juvena for me. That delay could have been fatal for all of us. It was more important to me that you and Kristen get home safe and let the authorities know about Celestica. I meant to tell you when you got back from dinner," said Harris. "I felt feverish, so I was going to take a bath in cold water, but the withdrawal reaction snuck up on me so quickly, I didn't even have a chance before I passed out."

"Well, thank God, it looks like you're going to be all right."

Harris smiled. "I knew I trained you to be a good doctor, and now I'm living proof. Bet my legs looked like pincushions."

Chad responded, "I wouldn't worry about that. You just won't wear shorts any time soon."

Dr. Creager stopped by and disconnected the VIP patient from cardiopulmonary bypass. His temperature remained in normal range as Chad tapered off the dose of Juvena, just as he had with the mice. Harris recovered, with no complications.

35

Kristen's story about Celestica appeared in the Sunday edition *Boston Globe* and simultaneously on its internet site. Monday morning, in Europe, the pharmaceutical company's stock price sank so precipitously the Zurich exchange had to halt trading in its shares. Bankers holding Celestica's debt went into a total frenzy. On the advice of his lawyer, Witig refused to grant interviews. He turned off his cell phone. During the dead of night, he stole away with Inger, nearly running over several reporters stationed around his house who tried to block his car's exit and speak with him. Witig headed straight for his chalet in Grindelwald.

The quaint mountain town of Grindelwald was the place where he felt most comfortable. Witig visited the small shop, now converted to a museum, where it had all begun with grandfather Anchel. He walked among the artifacts of the apothecary responsible for Celestica's birth. Then stepping outside, put his face in his hands, and cried.

Early the next morning, while Inger slept, Witig donned his mountaineering gear and went for a climb. On the way up the Wetterhorn, he stopped at three thousand meters to rest. Opening his backpack, he took out some cheese, and drank a little wine. Witig relished the vista that lay before him. Afterward, he continued his ascent toward the peak.

Being in superb condition, Witig had no problem with the climb. When he reached the top, he made a slow 360-degree turn, taking in the full magnificence of the view. It was a moment that brought him close to the essence of his being. Witig remembered Mount Everest, and an entry he had made in his journal:

With one final step that took all of my remaining strength, I made the summit. I removed my oxygen mask and took a deep breath of the frigid, thin air. My guide, Nygen, an experienced Sherpa, was with me. We were both were as close to heaven as men standing on earth can get. Nygen reached inside his jacket, took out a blue prayer scarf, and wrapped it around my neck, chanting a Tibetan prayer of thanksgiving. I placed my arm around Nygen's shoulder and, with my other hand, snapped a photo of the two of us smiling. For the next few minutes, I gloried in the radiance of the sun's pure rays at the top of the world.

That Everest climb seemed so long ago. Witig took off his backpack and mechanically reached inside. Gazing out at the Alps, he pressed the gun barrel against his temple and he pulled the trigger, sending fragments of skull and brain flying onto the mountain he so loved.

**

Six months later, Celestica was sold to the French concern, Sanofte. Gustav Jung had put in a low-ball bid for the company. He didn't think it worth as much as the French were willing to pay. Jung never raised his offer. The venerable Swiss company that had been built and run by a Witig since its inception was no more.

36

As he read the piece by Kristen Ross in the *Boston Globe*, Jim Anderson began to hyperventilate and have chest pain. His secretary called an ambulance, and he was taken to a hospital in Framingham. Anderson underwent an emergency cardiac procedure and had a stent placed in his coronary artery. After release, he was hounded by the press. Then a squadron of police cars showed up at the office with a warrant for his arrest. Anderson was charged with the unlawful detention of Dr. Harris, conspiracy to commit murder, and a host of other charges.

Before being taken away in handcuffs, he told the officer, "I've got severe diabetes, and need to take my special insulin." Anderson went to a refrigerator and the officer helped pack up his medication to take along. He had cleverly squirreled away dozens Juvena vials or his personal use and relabeled them as insulin, just in case.

In court, Anderson pleaded guilty and got a lesser sentence, claiming that his medical problems would kill him behind bars. In spite of that, the judge announced he would spend the next eight years in prison. Anderson was sent to a facility in Springfield, Massachusetts, but wasn't too distraught about the sentence. He reasoned that eight years from now he would be the same man, having not aged during his incarceration because of his Juvena injections.

As an inmate, Anderson received a daily dose from the vials kept in the prison infirmary refrigerator. The shots were administered by a certified medical technician. One day, the tech forgot to put the vial back in the refrigerator, leaving it out on a shelf exposed to direct sunlight. The next day he took Anderson's dose of 'special' insulin from the same vial, not thinking it would cause any problem. However, the DNA liposomes had denatured and were no longer biologically active. For several days, the tech continued drawing the injections from the vial of defective Juvena.

Three days later, Anderson began to feel warm, and thought he might be developing the flu. While he was walking in the prison yard, he fell to the ground and started convulsing. The grand mal seizures continued until the paramedics arrived, at which point his temperature was 105 degrees.

Anderson was transported to a local hospital. Doctors couldn't understand why his high fever wouldn't come down and in fact continued to rise. Bruises began to appear under Anderson's skin, all over his body. He vomited blood. Anderson briefly regained consciousness, but was delirious. The nurse thought she heard patient mumble something like *"juvenile... juvenile"* several times before slipping into a final deep coma. His last recorded temperature was 110 degrees. A few minutes before Anderson's monitor went flat-line, the nurse thought she detected the odor of something burning inside his room. Lifting the sheet that covered him, she saw smoke and was shocked to discover her patient's fingers and toes were charred, smoldering from self-combustion.

37

The patient was dressed and waiting for discharge when Chad stopped by his hospital room as he had every day during Harris's hospitalization. "Gordon, are you sure you're feeling up to leaving?" Chad asked.

"I walked around the ward ten times yesterday, and felt fine. I think I'm as ready as I'll ever be. Why don't you sign me out?"

"Well, since you're not a pediatric case, that's technically out of my jurisdiction. I'll have to leave it to your internist to give the official discharge order."

"So, Chad, did you see the paper today?" Harris handed him a copy of the *Globe* with a small headline below the fold: "Discredited Celestica CEO Commits Suicide."

Chad scanned the article. "Maybe he's in a better place now, but I'm awfully glad we're not there with him."

"I still need to get the rights to my DNA liposomes back. Let's not forget that."

"I haven't forgotten. In fact I've found just the right lawyer to handle your case, Pete Bullard. In legal circles, they call him Pit Bull."

Smiling, Harris exclaimed, "That sounds perfect!"

**

A few months later Chad saw Harris walking in the hospital corridor. He was carrying his signature old satchel briefcase.

Chad joked, "Gordon, don't you think with your settlement, you could afford to buy a new briefcase?" On Harris's behalf, his lawyer had signed a huge compensation award with Sanofte, the company that purchased Celestica and, unwittingly, assumed liability for what had happened to Harris.

"This briefcase is part of me," Harris said. "I'd just as soon lose a leg as part with it."

"Glad to see all those millions haven't changed you. Before I forget, Pete Bullard couriered this to the lab earlier. I stuck it in my pocket, thinking I'd drop it by your office later." Chad handed the envelope to Harris. It was a letter from Sanofte's CEO:

> *Dear Dr. Harris,*
>
> *This letter confirms that you retain exclusive rights to the use of the DNA liposomes formerly known as Juvena.*
>
> *I wish to express my sincere regret over the unfortunate nature of your dealings with Celestica. As you undoubtedly know, we recently purchased the company, and therefore assumed all its liabilities as well as its assets. One of those liabilities was the criminal maltreatment you experienced.*
>
> *In addition to the monetary settlement you have already received, please accept my enclosed personal donation of five-hundred thousand dollars. I hope you will use it toward establishing a dedicated progeria clinic at Boston General.*
>
> *With warm personal regards,*
> *Pierre Letierre*
> *CEO, Sanofte Pharmaceutical*

Harris handed the letter to Chad and watched his eyes widen as he read it. When he finished, Chad had a one-word comment. "Fantastic!"

**

One crisp fall day, Chad and Kristen paid Harris a surprise visit at his newly inaugurated progeria clinic. With his arm around Kristen, Chad said, "We wanted you to be the first to know about our engagement." He was beaming. "We're getting married this spring."

"That's wonderful!" Harris exclaimed.

"It would mean a lot to us if you would be part of our wedding party," said Kristen. "You really *are* the best man."

"I'd be honored," Harris said. "Even if Murdock was still chasing me, it wouldn't prevent me from being there." Then Harris reached into the pocket of his lab coat. He pulled out a card and said, "This is for both of you."

They looked at each other befuddled as Chad opened it and read aloud: *You two wonderful people are meant for each other. Have a long life of happiness and love together. Congratulations on your upcoming wedding.*

"What?" Chad exclaimed. How did you know?"

"There are no secrets from Miriam in this department. She dropped a hint to me about your good news."

Chad pulled out an enclosed check, his eyes widening as he looked at it. Then he passed it along to Kristen.

"Gordon we can't possibly accept this. It's enough for a down payment on a house!"

"That's precisely its intention. And let me say that if it wasn't for both of you, risking your lives to save my neck, I wouldn't be standing here in front of you today. Please accept my prenuptial gift."

**

The benefits from Juvena treatment were soon evident. Children who received the injections started changing before everyone's eyes. One of Harris's most advanced cases grew back lost hair. His painful arthritis improved and he threw away his cane. There were no reports of new heart attacks or strokes in any of the treated patients. Most of the patients getting the Juvena injections were able to start acting and playing like normal children for the first time in their lives. It was a dream come true for Harris's patients and their families.

Percy Adams, after recovering from his head injury, insisted on going back to work as soon as possible. As a season's first snow dusted the streets of Boston, a UPS truck delivered a package to the General's research building. Percy went down to pick it up.

When he returned, Percy spoke to Chad. "This just came by special delivery. Were you expecting something?"

"No, not that I can recall. Let's have a look."

Percy set the box down. Its mailing label read, "Biological Material; Handle with Care." The sender was listed as Sanofte Pharmaceutical. Percy opened the box, removing the top and peering inside. He turned to Chad, smiling, then lifted out a Plexiglas cube containing three mice.

"Holy shit!" Percy exclaimed. "These are Harris's miracle mice—the real ones."

Chad pulled out the enclosed note and read it aloud:

> Dear Dr. Reynolds,
> I apologize for the unfortunate delay in returning these mice. After Sanofte took control of Celestica, an audit of all inventories was performed. We found three mice that were unaccounted for in the records. It has taken until now for us to determine their origin, but we were eventually able to identify them as property of the research lab at Boston General.
> Best regards,
> Maurice D'Ardent
> Director of Research, Sanofte Pharmaceutical

Percy reflected for a moment, examining the mice more closely. Then he said, "You know, they haven't aged a bit since the last time I saw them. Do you suppose there is some lingering effect that slows aging even after injections with Juvena are tapered off? Maybe I'll start giving myself a daily shot of those DNA liposomes, beginning tomorrow."

Chad glared at Percy and barked. "Don't you dare!" before noticing the big grin on his tech's face. Percy started to laugh, softly at first, then progressively louder, until he held his sides. Although slow on the uptake, Chad soon joined in. The sound of their laughter echoed down the hallways of Boston General's research building.

**

Paul Holfield sat at his desk in the Novara headquarters. As the newly appointed director of drug development, his position was second only to the company's CEO, Gustav Jung. Holfield and Jung had become great friends. In fact, when Jung went on vacation, he put Holfield in charge of the entire Novara operation.

Holfield was happier than he'd ever been. He relished being king of Novara, even if it only lasted as long as it took Jung to return from a safari in Kenya or a trek at Katmandu. In addition to his generous salary, Holfield had carte blanche use of Jung's yacht and the company jet. He even had a burgeoning relationship with his administrative assistant, Inger Kroll, whom he had first met at Rolfe Witig's funeral.

One day Jung stuck his head into Holfield's office and said, "I'm planning on taking a month-long cruise of the orient, beginning next week. While I'm away, why don't you try and find us an American company that's worth acquiring?"

Holfield lit up at the prospect. In no time he had identified several American firms with promising drugs in their pipeline. When he thought about where to hold negotiations with representatives of the prospective companies, one place came to mind: Las Vegas.

Inger dialed the number Holfield had given her and was connected to the VIP desk at the Bellagio. "May we help you?" a pleasant voice asked.

"Yes, this is Mr. Holfield's office calling from Novara Pharmaceutical in Switzerland. I'd like to make reservations for a penthouse suite for three nights beginning next Thursday."

"Let me pull up a calendar to check availability."

While Inger was making the hotel reservations, Holfield sat in his office, thinking about the old days when he frequented sin city and enjoyed its excesses. Unfortunately, Inger didn't share his love of gambling but Holfield was certain he'd be able to find some time when he could hit the casinos on his own. Then he recalled Natalie, his favorite female companion in Vegas. Traveling with Inger would certainly complicate any rendezvous with the voluptuous woman he still dreamed about. There was also the issue of his true identity. As George Fleming, he was still wanted by Interpol, and even with his new face, Natalie might recognize him. Holfield closed his eyes and imagined the vixen's amazing body bouncing up and down atop his, then decided not to deprive himself.

Inger's voice came back on the intercom interrupting his reverie. "Darling, we have our penthouse suite confirmed at the Bellagio, just as you wanted."

"My love, I promise we will have a wonderful time on this trip. The best restaurants and entertainment in the world awaits us."

Getting off the intercom, he picked up his cell and scrolled to a number kept in its secure directory. A devilish grin slowly spread across Holfield's face as he dialed Natalie and waited for an answer.

32455051R00110

Made in the USA
Charleston, SC
19 August 2014